Nicole

W9-ADJ-382

Are You There God? It's Me, Margaret.

ARE YOU THERE GOD? IT'S ME, MARGARET.

By JUDY BLUME

BRADBURY PRESS Scarsdale, N.Y.

Copyright © 1970 by Judy Blume. All rights reserved.
No part of this book may be reproduced in any form or
by any means, except for the inclusion of brief quota-
tions in a review, without permission in writing from
the publisher. Library of Congress Catalog Card Number: 79–122741. Manufactured in the United States of
America.
ISBN 0-87888-022-4
10 9   79
The text of this book is set in 12pt. Electra.

To My Mother

Are you there God? It's me, Margaret. We're moving today. I'm so scared God. I've never lived anywhere but here. Suppose I hate my new school? Suppose everybody there hates me? Please help me God. Don't let New Jersey be too horrible. Thank you.

We moved on the Tuesday before Labor Day. I knew what the weather was like the second I got up. I knew because I caught my mother sniffing under her arms. She always does that when it's hot and humid, to make sure her deodorant's working. I don't use deodorant yet. I don't think people start to smell bad until they're at least twelve. So I've still got a few months to go.

I was really surprised when I came home from camp and found out our New York apartment had been rented to another family and that *we* owned a house in Farbrook, New Jersey. First of all I never even heard of Farbrook. And second of all, I'm not usually left out of important family decisions.

But when I groaned, "Why New Jersey?" I was told,

1

"Long Island is too social—Westchester is too expensive—and Connecticut is too inconvenient."

So Farbrook, New Jersey it was, where my father could commute to his job in Manhattan, where I could go to public school, and where my mother could have all the grass, trees and flowers she ever wanted. Except I never knew she wanted that stuff in the first place.

The new house is on Morningbird Lane. It isn't bad. It's part brick, part wood. The shutters and front door are painted black. Also, there is a very nice brass knocker. Every house on our new street looks a lot the same. They are all seven years old. So are the trees.

I think we left the city because of my grandmother, Sylvia Simon. I can't figure out any other reason for the move. Especially since my mother says Grandma is too much of an influence on me. It's no big secret in our family that Grandma sends me to summer camp in New Hampshire. And that she enjoys paying my private school tuition (which she won't be able to do any more because now I'll be going to public school). She even knits me sweaters that have labels sewed inside saying MADE EXPRESSLY FOR YOU . . . BY GRANDMA.

And she doesn't do all that because we're poor. I know for a fact that we're not. I mean, we aren't rich but we certainly have enough. Especially since I'm an only child. That cuts way down on food and clothes. I know this family that has seven kids and every time they go to the shoe store it costs a bundle. My mother and father didn't plan for me to be an only child, but that's the way it worked out, which is fine with me because this way I don't have anybody around to fight.

Anyhow, I figure this house-in-New-Jersey business is my parents' way of getting me away from Grandma. She doesn't have a car, she hates buses *and* she thinks all trains are dirty. So unless Grandma plans to walk, which is unlikely, I won't be seeing much of her. Now some kids might think, who cares about seeing a grandmother? But Sylvia Simon is a lot of fun, considering her age, which I happen to know is sixty. The only problem is she's always asking me if I have boyfriends and if they're Jewish. Now *that* is ridiculous because number one I don't have boyfriends. And number two what would I care if they're Jewish or not?

We hadn't been in the new house more than an hour when the doorbell rang. I answered. It was this girl in a bathing suit.

"Hi," she said. "I'm Nancy Wheeler. The real estate agent sent out a sheet on you. So I know you're Margaret and you're in sixth grade. So am I."

I wondered what else she knew.

"It's plenty hot, isn't it?" Nancy asked.

"Yes," I agreed. She was taller than me and had bouncy hair. The kind I'm hoping to grow. Her nose turned up so much I could look right into her nostrils.

Nancy leaned against the door. "Well, you want to come over and go under the sprinklers?"

"I don't know. I'll have to ask."

"Okay. I'll wait."

I found my mother with her rear end sticking out of a bottom kitchen cabinet. She was arranging her pots and pans.

"Hey Mom. There's a girl here who wants to know if I can go under her sprinklers?"

"If you want to," my mother said.

"I need my bathing suit," I said.

"Gads, Margaret! I don't know where a bathing suit is in this mess."

I walked back to the front door and told Nancy, "I can't find my bathing suit."

"You can borrow one of mine," she said.

"Wait a second," I said, running back to the kitchen. "Hey Mom. She says I can wear one of hers. Okay?"

"Okay," my mother mumbled from inside the cabinet. Then she backed out. She spit her hair out of her face. "What did you say her name was?"

"Umm . . . Wheeler. Nancy Wheeler."

"Okay. Have a good time," my mother said.

Nancy lives six houses away, also on Morningbird Lane. Her house looks like mine but the brick is painted white and the front door and shutters are red.

"Come on in," Nancy said.

I followed her into the foyer, then up the four stairs leading to the bedrooms. The first thing I noticed about Nancy's room was the dressing table with the heartshaped mirror over it. Also, everything was very neat.

When I was little I wanted a dressing table like that. The kind that's wrapped up in a fluffy organdy skirt. I never got one though, because my mother likes tailored things.

Nancy opened her bottom dresser drawer. "When's your birthday?" she asked.

5

"March," I told her.

"Great! We'll be in the same class. There are three sixth grades and they arrange us by age. I'm April."

"Well, I don't know what class I'm in but I know it's Room Eighteen. They sent me a lot of forms to fill out last week and that was printed on all of them."

"I told you we'd be together. I'm in Room Eighteen too." Nancy handed me a yellow bathing suit. "It's clean," she said. "My mother always washes them after a wearing."

"Thank you," I said, taking the suit. "Where should I change?"

Nancy looked around the room. "What's wrong with here?"

"Nothing," I said. "I don't mind if you don't mind."

"Why should I mind?"

"I don't know." I worked the suit on from the bottom. I knew it was going to be too big. Nancy gave me the creeps the way she sat on her bed and watched me. I left my polo on until the last possible second. I wasn't about to let her see I wasn't growing yet. That was my business.

"Oh, you're still flat." Nancy laughed.

"Not exactly," I said, pretending to be very cool. "I'm small boned, is all."

"I'm growing already," Nancy said, sticking her chest way out. "In a few years I'm going to look like one of those girls in *Playboy*."

Well, I didn't think so, but I didn't say anything. My father gets *Playboy* and I've seen those girls in the middle. Nancy looked like she had a long way to go. Almost as far as me.

"Want me to do up your straps?" she asked.

"Okay."

"I figured you'd be real grown up coming from New York. City girls are supposed to grow up a lot faster. Did you ever kiss a boy?"

"You mean really kiss? On the lips?" I asked.

"Yes," Nancy said impatiently. "Did you?"

"Not really," I admitted.

Nancy breathed a sigh of relief. "Neither did I."

I was overjoyed. Before she said that I was beginning to feel like some kind of underdeveloped little kid.

"I practice a lot though," Nancy said.

"Practice what?" I asked.

"Kissing! Isn't that what we were talking about? *Kissing!*"

"How can you practice that?" I asked.

"Watch this." Nancy grabbed her bed pillow and embraced it. She gave it a long kiss. When she was done she threw the pillow back on the bed. "It's important to experiment, so when the time comes you're all ready. I'm going to be a great kisser some day. Want to see something else?"

I just stood there with my mouth half open. Nancy

sat down at her dressing table and opened a drawer. "Look at this," she said.

I looked. There were a million little bottles, jars and tubes. There were more cosmetics in that drawer than my mother had all together. I asked, "What do you do with all that stuff?"

"It's another one of my experiments. To see how I look best. So when the time comes I'll be ready." She opened a lipstick and painted on a bright pink mouth. "Well, what do you think?"

"Umm . . . I don't know. It's kind of bright, isn't it?"

Nancy studied herself in the heartshaped mirror. She rubbed her lips together. "Well, maybe you're right." She wiped off the lipstick with a tissue. "My mother would kill me if I came out like this anyway. I can't wait till eighth grade. That's when I'll be allowed to wear lipstick every day."

Then she whipped out a hairbrush and started to brush her long, brown hair. She parted it in the middle and caught it at the back with a barrette. "Do you always wear your hair like that?" she asked me.

My hand went up to the back of my neck. I felt all the bobby pins I'd used to pin my hair up so my neck wouldn't sweat. I knew it looked terrible. "I'm letting it grow," I said. "It's at that in-between stage now. My mother thinks I should wear it over my ears though. My ears stick out a little."

"I noticed," Nancy said.

I got the feeling that Nancy noticed *everything!*

"Ready to go?" she asked.

"Sure."

She opened a linen closet in the hall and handed me a purple towel. I followed her down the stairs and into the kitchen, where she grabbed two peaches out of the refrigerator and handed one to me. "Want to meet my mom?" she asked.

"Okay," I said, taking a bite of my peach.

"She's thirty-eight, but tells us she's twenty-five. Isn't that a scream!" Nancy snorted.

Mrs. Wheeler was on the porch with her legs tucked under her and a book on her lap. I couldn't tell what book it was. She was suntanned and had the same nose as Nancy.

"Mom, this is Margaret Simon who just moved in down the street."

Mrs. Wheeler took off her glasses and smiled at me.

"Hello," I said.

"Hello, Margaret. I'm very glad to meet you. You're from New York, aren't you?"

"Yes, I am."

"East side or West?"

"We lived on West Sixty-seventh. Near Lincoln Center."

"How nice. Does your father still work in the city?"

"Yes."

"And what does he do?"

"He's in insurance." I sounded like a computer.

"How nice. Please tell your mother I'm looking forward to meeting her. We've got a Morningbird Lane bowling team on Mondays and a bridge game every other Thursday afternoon and a . . ."

"Oh, I don't think my mother knows how to bowl and she wouldn't be interested in bridge. She paints most of the day," I explained.

"She paints?" Mrs. Wheeler asked.

"Yes."

"How interesting. What does she paint?"

"Mostly pictures of fruits and vegetables. Sometimes flowers too."

Mrs. Wheeler laughed. "Oh, you mean *pictures!* I thought you meant walls! Tell your mother we're making our car pools early this year. We'd be happy to help her arrange hers . . . especially Sunday school. That's always the biggest problem."

"I don't go to Sunday school."

"You don't?"

"No."

"*Lucky!*" Nancy shouted.

"Nancy, *please!*" Mrs. Wheeler said.

"Hey Mom . . . Margaret came to go under the sprinkler with me, not to go through the third degree."

"All right. If you see Evan tell him I want to talk to him."

Nancy grabbed me by the hand and pulled me outside. "I'm sorry my mother's so nosey."

"I didn't mind," I said. "Who's Evan?"

10

"He's my brother. He's disgusting!"

"Disgusting how?" I asked.

"Because he's fourteen. All boys of fourteen are disgusting. They're only interested in two things—pictures of naked girls and dirty books!"

Nancy really seemed to know a lot. Since I didn't know any boys of fourteen I took her word for it.

Nancy turned on the outside faucet and adjusted it so that the water sprayed lightly from the sprinkler. "Follow the leader!" she called, running through the water. I guessed Nancy was the leader.

She jumped through the spray. I followed. She turned cartwheels. I tried but didn't make it. She did leaps through the air. I did too. She stood straight under the spray. I did the same. That's when the water came on full blast. We both got drenched, including our hair.

"Evan, you stinker!" Nancy shrieked. "I'm telling!" She ran off to the house and left me alone with two boys.

"Who're you?" Evan asked.

"I'm Margaret. We just moved in."

"Oh. This is Moose," he said, pointing to the other boy.

I nodded.

"Hey," Moose said. "If you just moved in, ask your father if he's interested in having me cut his lawn. Five bucks a week and I trim too. What'd you say your last name was?"

11

"I didn't. But it's Simon." I couldn't help thinking about what Nancy said—that all they were interested in was dirty books and naked girls. I held my towel tight around me in case they were trying to sneak a look down my bathing suit.

"*Evan! Come in here this instant!*" Mrs. Wheeler hollered from the porch.

"I'm coming . . . I'm coming," Evan muttered.

After Evan went inside Moose said, "Don't forget to tell your father. *Moose Freed.* I'm in the phone book."

"I won't forget," I promised.

Moose nibbled a piece of grass. Then the back door slammed and Nancy came out, red-eyed and sniffling.

"Hey, Nancy baby! Can't you take a joke?" Moose asked.

"Shut up, animal!" Nancy yelled. Then she turned to me. "I'm sorry they had to act like that on your first day here. Come on, I'll walk you home."

Nancy had my clothes wrapped up in a little bundle. She was still in her wet suit. She pointed out who lived in each house between mine and hers.

"We're going to the beach for Labor Day weekend," she said. "So call for me on the first day of school and we'll walk together. I'm absolutely dying to know who our teacher's going to be. Miss Phipps, who we were supposed to have, ran off with some guy to California last June. So we're getting somebody new."

When we got to my house I told Nancy if she'd wait a minute I'd give her back her bathing suit.

12

"I don't need it in a hurry. Tell your mother to wash it and you can give it back next week. It's an old one."

I was sorry she told me that. Even if I'd already guessed it. I mean, probably I wouldn't lend a stranger my best bathing suit either. But I wouldn't come right out and say it.

"Oh, listen, Margaret," Nancy said. "On the first day of school wear loafers, but no socks."

"How come?"

"Otherwise you'll look like a baby."

"Oh."

"Besides, I want you to join my secret club and if you're wearing socks the other kids might not want you."

"What kind of secret club?" I asked.

"I'll tell you about it when school starts."

"Okay," I said.

"And remember—no socks!"

"I'll remember."

We went to a hamburger place for supper. I told my father about Moose Freed. "Only five bucks a cutting and he trims too."

"No, thanks," my father said. "I'm looking forward to cutting it myself. That's one of the reasons we moved out here. Gardening is good for the soul." My mother beamed. They were really driving me crazy with all that good-for-the-soul business. I wondered when they became such nature lovers!

13

Later, when I was getting ready for bed, I walked into a closet, thinking it was the bathroom. Would I ever get used to living in this house? When I finally made it into bed and turned out the light, I saw shadows on my wall. I tried to shut my eyes and not think about them but I kept checking to see if they were still there. I couldn't fall asleep.

Are you there God? It's me, Margaret. I'm in my new bedroom but I still have the same bed. It's so quiet here at night—nothing like the city. I see shadows on my wall and hear these funny creaking sounds. It's scary God! Even though my father says all houses make noises and the shadows are only trees. I hope he knows what he's talking about! I met a girl today. Her name's Nancy. She expected me to be very grown up. I think she was disappointed. Don't you think it's time for me to start growing God? If you could arrange it I'd be very glad. Thank you.

My parents don't know I actually talk to God. I mean, if I told them they'd think I was some kind of religious fanatic or something. So I keep it very private. I can talk to him without moving my lips if I have to. My mother says God is a nice idea. He belongs to everybody.

14

3

The next day we went to the hardware store where my father bought a deluxe power lawn mower. That evening, after our first at-home-in-New-Jersey supper (turkey sandwiches from the local delicatessen), my father went out to cut the grass with his new mower. He did fine on the front, but when he got around to the back yard he had to check to see how much grass there was in the bag on the mower. It's a very simple thing to do. The man at the hardware store demonstrated just how to do it. Only you have to turn the mower off before you reach inside and my father forgot that.

I heard him yell, "Barbara—I've had an accident!" He ran to the house. He grabbed a towel and wrapped it around his hand before I had a chance to see anything. Then he sat down on the floor and turned very pale.

"Oh my God!" my mother said when the blood seeped through the towel. "Did you cut it off?"

When I heard that I raced outside to look for the limb. I didn't know if they were talking about the whole hand or what, but I had read about how you're supposed to save limbs if they get cut off because some-times the doctor can sew them back on. I thought it was a good thing they had me around to think of those things. But I couldn't find a hand or any fingers and by the time I came back into the house the police were there. My mother was on the floor too, with my father's head in her lap.

I rode in the police car with them since there was no one at home to stay with me. I had a silent talk with God on the way to the hospital. I said this inside my head so no one would notice.

Are you there God? It's me, Margaret. My father's had an awful accident. Please help him God. He's really very kind and nice. Even though he doesn't know you the way I do, he's a good father. And he needs his hand God. So please, please let him be all right. I'll do anything you say if you help him. Thank you God.

It turned out that my father hadn't cut off anything. but it took eight stitches to sew up his finger. The doc-tor who sewed him was Dr. Potter. After he was through with my father, he came out to chat. When he saw me he said, "I have a daughter about your age."

I love the way people always think they know some-body your age until you tell them how old you *really* are!

"I'm going on twelve," I said.

"Gretchen is almost twelve too," the doctor said.

Well! He was right about my age.

"She'll be in sixth grade at Delano School."

"So will you, Margaret," my mother reminded me. As if I needed reminding.

"I'll tell Gretchen to look for you," Dr. Potter said.

"Fine," I told him.

As soon as we got home from the hospital my father told my mother to look up Moose Freed in the phone book and arrange for him to cut our lawn once a week.

On Labor Day I got up early. I wanted to fix up my desk in my room before school started. I'd bought a pile of paper, pencils, erasers, reinforcements and paper clips. I'm always real neat until about October. While I was in the middle of this project I heard a noise. It sounded like somebody knocking. I waited to see if my parents would wake up. I tiptoed to their room but the door was still closed and it was quiet so I knew they were asleep.

When I heard the knocking again I went downstairs to investigate. I wasn't scared because I knew I could always scream and my father would rescue me if it turned out to be a burglar or a kidnapper.

The knocking came from the front door. Nancy was away for the weekend so it couldn't be her. And we really didn't know anybody else.

"Who is it?" I asked, pressing my ear to the door.

"It's Grandma, Margaret. Open up."

I unlatched the chain and both locks and flung open the door. "Grandma! I can't believe it. You're really here!"

"Surprise!" Grandma called.

I put a finger over my lips to let her know my parents were still asleep.

Grandma was loaded down with Bloomingdale's shopping bags. But when she stepped into the house she lined them up on the floor and gave me a big hug and kiss.

"My Margaret!" she said, flashing her special smile. When she smiles like that she shows all her top teeth. They aren't her real teeth. It's what Grandma calls a bridge. She can take out a whole section of four top teeth when she wants to. She used to entertain me by doing that when I was little. Naturally I never told my parents. When she smiles without her teeth in place she looks like a witch. But with them in her mouth she's very pretty.

"Come on, Margaret. Let's get these bags into the kitchen."

I picked up one shopping bag. "Grandma, this is so heavy! What's in it?"

"Hotdogs, potato salad, cole slaw, corned beef, rye bread. . . ."

I laughed. "You mean it's food?"

"Of course it's food."

"But they have food in New Jersey, Grandma."

"Not this kind."

"Oh yes," I said. "Even delicatessen."

"No place has delicatessen like New York!"

I didn't argue about that. Grandma has certain ideas of her own.

When we got all the bags into the kitchen Grandma scrubbed her hands at the sink and put everything into the refrigerator.

When she was done I asked, "How did you get here?"

Grandma smiled again but didn't say anything. She was measuring coffee into the pot. You can't make her talk about something until she's ready.

Finally she sat down at the kitchen table, fluffed out her hair and said, "I came in a taxi."

"All the way from New York?"

"No," Grandma said. "From the center of Farbrook."

"But how did you get to the center of Farbrook?"

"On a train."

"Oh, Grandma—you didn't!"

"Yes, I did."

"But you always said trains are so dirty!"

"So what's a little dirt? I'm washable!"

We both laughed while Grandma changed her shoes. She brought a spare pair along with her knitting in one of the shopping bags.

"Now," she said, "take me on a tour of the house."

I led her everywhere except upstairs. I pointed out closets, the downstairs bathroom, my mother's new washer and dryer, and where we sat to watch TV.

When I was finished Grandma shook her head and said, "I just don't understand why they had to move to the country."

"It's not really country, Grandma," I explained. "There aren't any cows around."

"To me it's country!" Grandma said.

I heard the water running upstairs. "I think they're up. Should I go see?"

"You mean should you go *tell!*"

"Well, should I?"

"Of course," Grandma said.

I ran up the stairs and into my parents' bedroom. My father was putting on his socks. My mother was brushing her teeth in their bathroom.

"Guess who's here?" I said to my father.

He didn't say anything. He yawned.

"Well, aren't you going to guess?"

"Guess what?" he asked.

"Guess who's here in this very house at this very minute?"

"Nobody but us, I hope," my father said.

"Wrong!" I danced around the bedroom.

"Margaret," my father said in his disgusted-with-me voice. "What is it you're trying to say?"

"Grandma's here!"

"That's impossible," my father told me.

"I mean it, Daddy. She's right downstairs in the kitchen making your coffee."

"Barbara . . ." My father went into the bathroom and turned off the water. I followed him. My mother had a mouthful of toothpaste.

"I'm not done, Herb," she said, turning on the water again.

My father shut it off. "Guess who's here?" he asked her.

"What do you mean who's here?" my mother said.

"Sylvia! That's who's here!" My father turned the water back on so my mother could finish brushing her teeth.

But my mother turned it off and followed my father into the bedroom. I followed too. This was fun! I guess by then my mother must have swallowed her toothpaste.

"What do you mean, *Sylvia?*" my mother asked my father.

"I mean my *mother!*" my father said.

My mother laughed. "That's impossible, Herb. How would she even get here?"

My father pointed at me. "Ask Margaret. She seems to know everything."

"In a taxi," I said.

They didn't say anything.

"And a train," I said.

Still nothing.

"It wasn't so dirty after all."

Ten minutes later my mother and father joined Grandma in the kitchen where the table was set and the breakfast all ready. It's hard to get mad at Grandma, especially when she flashes her super smile. So my mother and father didn't say anything except what a wonderful surprise! And how clever of Grandma to take a train and a taxi to our new house when she'd never been to Farbrook before.

After breakfast I went upstairs to get dressed. Grandma came up with me to see my room.

"It's a lot bigger than my old one," I said.

"Yes, it's bigger," Grandma agreed. "You could use new bedspreads and curtains. I saw some the other day—pink and red plaid. Then we could get red carpeting to match and a———" Grandma sighed. "But I guess your mother wants to fix it up herself."

"I guess so," I said.

Grandma sat down on my bed. "Margaret darling," she said, "I want to make sure you understand that we'll still be as close as always."

"Of course we will," I said.

"A few miles doesn't mean a thing," Grandma said. "Just because I can't drop in after school doesn't mean I won't think of you every day."

"I know that, Grandma."

"I tell you what—I'll call you every night at seven-thirty. How does that sound?"

"You don't have to call *every* night," I said.

"I want to! It's my dime," Grandma laughed. "That

22

way you can tell me what's going on and I'll keep you posted about New York. Okay?"

"Sure Grandma."

"But Margaret . . ."

"What?"

"You answer the phone. Your mother and father might not like me calling so much. This is just between you and me. All right?"

"Sure, Grandma. I love to get phone calls."

We all spent the rest of the day sitting around in our yard. Grandma was knitting me a new sweater, my mother planted some fall flowers, and my father read a book. I sunbathed, thinking it would be nice to start school with a tan.

We ate Grandma's food for supper and every time she bit into a pickle she said, "Mmm . . . nothing like the real thing!"

We drove her back to the Farbrook station while it was still light. Grandma has this thing about walking in New York at night. She's positive she's going to get mugged. Before she got out of the car she kissed me good-by and told my parents, "Now don't worry. I promise I'll only come once a month. Well . . . maybe twice. And it's not to see you, Herb. Or you either, Barbara. I've got to keep an eye on my Margaret—that's all." Grandma winked at me.

With that she grabbed the shopping bag with her shoes and knitting and left, waving good-by until we couldn't see her anymore.

4

On Wednesday night my mother helped me wash my hair. She set it in big rollers for me. I planned to sleep like that all night but after an hour they hurt my head so I took them out. On Thursday morning I got up early but I had trouble eating. My mother said it was natural for me to feel uneasy on the first day of school. She said when she was a girl she felt the same way. My mother's always telling me about when she was a girl. It's supposed to make me feel that she understands everything.

I put on my new blue plaid cotton back-to-school dress. My mother likes me in blue. She says it brings out the color in my eyes. I wore my brown loafers without socks. My mother thought that was dumb.

"Margaret, you have to walk three quarters of a mile."

"So?"

"So, you know you get blisters every time you go without socks."

"Well then, I'll just have to suffer."

"But why suffer? Wear socks!"

Now that's my point about my mother. I mean, if she understands so much about me then why couldn't she understand that I had to wear loafers without socks? I told her, "Nancy says nobody in the sixth grade wears socks on the first day of school!"

"Margaret! I don't know what I'm going to do with you when you're a teenager if you're acting like this now!"

That's another thing. My mother's always talking about when I'm a teenager. Stand up straight, Margaret! Good posture now makes for a good figure later. Wash your face with soap, Margaret! Then you won't get pimples when you're a teenager. If you ask me, being a teenager is pretty rotten—between pimples and worrying about how you smell!

Finally my mother told me to have a good day. She kissed my cheek and gave me a pat on the back. I walked down to Nancy's house.

By the time I got to Room Eighteen of the Delano Elementary School my feet hurt so much I thought I wouldn't make it through the day. Why are mothers always right about those things? As it turned out, half the girls had on knee socks anyway.

The teacher wasn't in the room when we got there. That is, the *real* teacher. There was this girl, who I thought *was* the teacher, but she turned out to be a kid in our class. She was very tall (that's why I thought she was the teacher) with eyes shaped like a cat's. You could see the outline of her bra through her blouse and you could also tell from the front that it wasn't the smallest size. She sat down alone and didn't talk to anyone. I wondered if maybe she was new too, because everybody else was busy talking and laughing about summer vacations and new hair styles and all that.

The class quieted down in a big hurry when a man walked into the room, nodded at us and wrote a name on the blackboard.

MILES J. BENEDICT JR.

When he turned away from the blackboard he cleared his throat. "That's me," he said, pointing to the name on the board. Then he cleared his throat two more times. "I'm your new teacher."

Nancy poked me in the ribs and whispered, "Can you believe it?" The whole class was whispering and grinning.

Mr. Benedict went back to the board. He wrote six phrases. Then he turned to us. He put his hands behind his back and kind of rocked back and forth on his feet. He cleared his throat so I knew he was going to say something.

"Now then . . . uh . . . you know my name. I'll tell you something about myself. Uh . . . I'm twenty-four years old. I'm uh . . . a graduate of Columbia Teachers College and uh . . . this is my first teaching position. Now that you know about me, I want to uh . . . find out about you. So, if you will copy these six phrases off the board and then complete them I'd uh . . . appreciate it. Thank you." He coughed. I thought he was going to wind up with a very sore throat.

Mr. Benedict Jr. handed out the paper himself. I read his phrases.

MY NAME IS
PLEASE CALL ME
I LIKE
I HATE
THIS YEAR IN SCHOOL
I THINK MALE TEACHERS ARE

I nibbled on the edge of my pencil. The first two were easy. I wrote:

My name is Margaret Ann Simon.
Please call me Margaret.

The next two were harder. I liked and hated a million things. And I didn't know what he wanted to know about. Also, he wouldn't answer any questions. He sat at his desk and watched us. He tapped his fingers and crossed his legs. Finally I wrote:

I like long hair, tuna fish, the smell of rain
and things that are pink.
I hate pimples, baked potatoes, when my

27

mother's mad and religious holidays.
This year in school I want to have fun.
And also learn enough to go to
seventh grade.
I think male teachers are . . .

That was the worst! How was I supposed to know?
Every teacher is different. But I couldn't think of a
way to fit that in. So I wrote:

I think male teachers are the opposite of
female teachers.

There! That ought to do it. It was a stupid answer
but I thought it was also a pretty stupid question.

At two-thirty Nancy slipped me a note. It said:
*Secret club meets today after school my house—no
socks!*

I went home to change before going to Nancy's. My
mother was waiting for me. "Let's have a snack and
you can tell me all about your first day of school," she
said.

"I can't," I told her. "No time now. I've got to go
to Nancy's house. I'm joining her secret club."

"Oh, that's nice," my mother said. "Just tell me
about your teacher. What's she like?"

"It's a *he*," I said. "His name is Mr. Benedict and
this is his first job."

"Oh gads! A first-year teacher. What could be worse?"

"He's not bad," I told my mother. "I thought he was very nice."

"We'll see how much you learn," my mother said.

I changed into shorts and a polo and walked to Nancy's.

5

The others were already there. Janie Loomis, Gretchen Potter and Nancy. That was it. We sat around on the porch and Nancy brought us cokes and cookies. When Gretchen helped herself to six Oreos at once Nancy asked her how much weight she'd gained over the summer. Gretchen put back four cookies and said, "Not much."

"Did you see Laura Danker come in this morning?" Janie asked.

"Which one is she?" I said.

They all giggled. Nancy spoke to me as if she were my mother. "Margaret dear—you can't possibly miss Laura Danker. The big blonde with the big *you know whats!*"

"Oh, I noticed her right off," I said. "She's very pretty."

"Pretty!" Nancy snorted. "You be smart and stay away from her. She's got a bad reputation."

"What do you mean?" I asked.

"My brother says she goes behind the A&P with him and Moose."

"And," Janie added, "she's been wearing a bra since fourth grade and I'll bet she gets her period."

"Did you get it yet, Margaret?" Nancy asked.

"Get what?"

"Your period," Nancy said, like I should have known.

"Oh—no, not yet. Did you?"

Nancy swallowed some soda and shook her head. "None of us has yet."

I was glad to hear that. I mean, suppose they all got it already and I was the only one who didn't. I'd feel awful.

Gretchen smacked her lips, brushed the cookie crumbs off her lap and said, "Let's get down to business."

"Agreed," Nancy said. "First of all we need a good club name this year. Everybody think up a name for our club."

It got quiet. Everybody thought. I didn't really think but I pretended to. I didn't even know anything about the club so how could I pick out a name?

Gretchen suggested the SGCT which meant the Sixth Grade Cu-Tees. Janie said that sounded really dumb. So Grechen told Janie if she was so smart why didn't she suggest a name. Janie suggested the MJB Girls which meant the Miles J. Benedict Girls. Nancy told Janie she'd forgotten the Jr. on the end of his name. Janie got mad and excused herself to go to the bathroom.

"As long as we're on the subject," Nancy said, "what do you think of Miles J.?"

"I think he's cute!" Gretchen giggled.

"He is—but he's too skinny," Nancy said.

Then I finally thought of something to say. "I wonder if he's married!"

Janie joined us again. "My guess is no. He doesn't look married."

"Anyhow, did you see the way he looked at Laura?" Nancy asked.

"No! Did he?" Gretchen opened her eyes wide.

"Naturally! Men can't help looking at her," Nancy said.

"But do you think she looks that way on purpose?" I asked.

The others laughed and Nancy said, "Oh Margaret!" Nancy had a great way of making me feel like a dope.

Then we talked about Mr. Benedict's questions and Gretchen told us that she wrote male teachers are very strict—because if Mr. Benedict thought we were afraid of him he'd bend over backwards to be really easy going and nice. I thought that was pretty clever and wished I had written it myself.

"Well, the whole idea of those questions is just to find out if we're normal," Janie said.

I hadn't thought about that. Now it was too late. "How can he tell if we're normal?" I asked.

"That's easy," Nancy said. "From the way you answered. Like if you said, I hate my mother, my father and my brother, you might be weird. Get it?"

I got it.

Nancy snapped her fingers. "I have the perfect name for our club," she said.

"What is it?" Gretchen asked.

"Tell us," Janie said.

"We'll be the Four PTS's."

"What's it stand for?" Janie asked.

Nancy tossed her hair around and smiled. "The Pre-Teen Sensations!"

"Hey, that's good," Gretchen said.

"I love it," Janie squealed.

We had a secret vote to pass the club name and naturally it passed. Then Nancy decided we should all have secret sensational names such as Alexandra, Veronica, Kimberly and Mavis. Nancy got to be Alexandra. I was Mavis.

Nancy reminded us that nobody in school was to know anything about our secret club and that at secret meetings such as this we were to use our secret names. We all had to solemnly swear. Then we all had to think up a rule.

Nancy's rule was, we all had to wear bras. I felt my cheeks turn red. I wondered if the others wore them already. I didn't think Janie did because she looked down at the floor after Nancy said it.

Gretchen's rule was, the first one to get her period had to tell the others all about it. Especially how it feels. Janie's rule was, we all had to keep a Boy Book, which was a notebook with a list of boys' names in

33

order of how we liked them. Each week we had to change our lists and pass the Boy Books around.

Finally Nancy asked me what my rule was. I couldn't think of one to equal the others so I said, "We meet on a certain day each week."

"Naturally!" Nancy said. "But *what* day?"

"Well, I don't know," I told her.

"Okay, let's think up a good day," Gretchen said. "Tuesday and Thursday are out. I have to go to Hebrew school."

"Oh Gretchen!" Janie said. "You and that Hebrew school business. Can't you get out of it?"

"I'd love to," Gretchen explained. "But I've got to go one more year and then I'm through."

"What about you, Margaret? Do you go?" Janie asked me.

"You mean to Hebrew school?"

"Yes."

"No, I don't go," I said.

"Margaret doesn't even go to Sunday school. Isn't that right?" Nancy asked.

"Yes," I answered.

"How'd you arrange that?" Gretchen asked.

"I'm not any religion," I said.

"You're not!" Gretchen's mouth fell open.

"What are your parents?" Janie asked.

"Nothing," I said.

"How positively neat!" Gretchen said.

Then they all just looked at me and nobody said

anything and I felt pretty silly. So I tried to explain. "See uh . . . my father was Jewish and uh . . . my mother was Christian and . . ."

Nancy's face lit up. "Go on," she said.

This was the first time they were interested in anything I had to say. "Well, my mother's parents, who live in Ohio, told her they didn't want a Jewish son-in-law. If she wanted to ruin her life that was her business. But they would never accept my father for her husband."

"No kidding!" Gretchen said. "How about your father's family?"

"Well, my grandmother wasn't happy about getting a Christian daughter-in-law, but she at least accepted the situation."

"So what happened?" Janie asked.

"They eloped."

"How romantic!" Nancy sighed.

"So that's why they're not anything."

"I don't blame them," Gretchen said. "I wouldn't be either."

"But if you aren't any religion, how are you going to know if you should join the Y or the Jewish Community Center?" Janie asked.

"I don't know," I said. "I never thought about it. Maybe we won't join either one."

"But *everybody* belongs to one or the other," Nancy said.

"Well, I guess that will be up to my parents," I said,

ready to change the subject. I never meant to tell them my story in the first place. "So uh . . . what day should we meet?"

Nancy announced that Friday was no good for a meeting day because she had piano lessons. Janie said she had ballet on Wednesday so I said that only left Mondays and we agreed that Monday would be our meeting day. Next week we had to bring our Boy Books and get checked to make sure we were all wearing bras.

When the meeting was over Nancy raised her arms high above her head. She closed her eyes and whispered, "Here's to the Four PTS's. Hurray!"

"Long live the PTS's," we chanted.

All through supper I thought about how I was going to tell my mother I wanted to wear a bra. I wondered why she hadn't ever asked me if I wanted one, since she knew so much about being a girl.

When she came in to kiss me goodnight I said it. "I want to wear a bra." Just like that—no beating around the bush.

My mother turned the bedroom light back on. "Margaret . . . how come?"

"I just do is all." I hid under the covers so she couldn't see my face.

My mother took a deep breath. "Well, if you really want to we'll have to go shopping on Saturday. Okay?"

36

"Okay." I smiled. My mother wasn't bad.

She turned out the light and closed my door half-way. Was I glad that was over!

Are you there God? It's me, Margaret. I just told my mother I want a bra. Please help me grow God. You know where. I want to be like every-one else. You know God, my new friends all be-long to the Y or the Jewish Community Center. Which way am I supposed to go? I don't know what you want me to do about that.

6

The next day after school Mr. Benedict called me up to his desk. "Margaret," he said. "I'd like to discuss your getting-to-know-you paper. For instance, why do you hate religious holidays?"

Was I sorry I wrote that! How positively stupid of me. If it was true that he was trying to find out if we were normal, I guess he thought I wasn't.

I half laughed. "Oh, I just wrote that," I said. "I really don't hate them at all."

"You must have had a reason. You can tell me. It's confidential."

I raised my right eyebrow at Mr. Benedict. I can do that really good. Raise one without the other. I do it whenever I can't think of anything to say. People notice it right away. Some people actually ask me how I do it. They forget what we were talking about and concentrate on my right eyebrow. I don't know exactly how I do it. What I do is think about it and the eyebrow goes up. I can't do it with my left. Only my right.

Mr. Benedict noticed. But he didn't ask me anything about how I do it. He just said, "I'm sure you have a perfectly good reason for hating religious holidays."

I knew he was waiting for me to say something. He wasn't going to just forget about it. So I decided to get it over with in a hurry. "None of those holidays are special to me. I don't belong to any religion," I said.

Mr. Benedict seemed pleased. Like he had un- covered some deep, dark mystery. "I see. And your parents?"

"They aren't any religion. I'm supposed to choose my own when I grow up. If I want to, that is."

Mr. Benedict folded his hands and looked at me for a while. Then he said, "Okay, Margaret. You can go now."

I hoped he decided I was normal, after all. I lived in New York for eleven and a half years and I don't think anybody ever asked me about my religion. I never even thought about it. Now, all of a sudden, it was the big thing in my life.

That night when Grandma called she told me she'd gotten a subscription to Lincoln Center for the two of us. We'd meet one Saturday a month, have lunch and then go to a concert. Grandma really is clever. She knew my parents would never say no to one Saturday a month at Lincoln Center. That was culture. And they thought culture was very important. And now Grandma and I would have a chance to spend some time alone. But I was glad that Lincoln Center didn't start right away because I didn't want anything to interfere with Bra Day.

First thing on Saturday morning Moose Freed arrived to cut our lawn. My father sulked behind a sports magazine. His finger was a lot better but it was still bandaged.

I sat around outside while Moose cut the grass. I liked the way he sang as he worked. I also liked his teeth. I saw them when he smiled at me. They were very clean and white and one in the front was a little crooked. I pretended to be really busy reading a book but the truth is—I was watching Moose. If he looked toward me I put my nose back in the book in a hurry. Moose would be number one in my Boy Book if only I was brave enough, but what would Nancy think? She hated him.

After lunch my mother told my father we were going shopping. We still had our same car but my mother thought we needed two now, because there weren't any buses in Farbrook and taxis were so expensive. My father said he'd see, but I knew we'd be getting another one soon. My mother can talk my father into anything.

My mother drove to a shopping center where there was a Lord & Taylor. I had on my blue plaid dress and my loafers without socks and three Bandaids on my blisters.

First we went to the ladies' lingerie department where my mother told the saleslady we wanted to see a bra for me. The saleslady took one look and told my mother we'd be better off in the teen department where they had bras in very small sizes. My mother thanked the lady and I almost died! We went down on the escalator and headed for the teen shop. They had a whole display of underwear there. Bras and panties and slips to match. All I ever wore was white underpants and regular undershirts. Sometimes a slip if I was going to a party. My mother went to the counter and told the saleslady we were interested in a bra. I stood back and pretended not to know a thing. I even bent down to scratch a new mosquito bite.

"Come here, dear," the saleslady called.

I hate people who call you dear. I walked over to the counter and raised my right eyebrow at her.

She reached over the top of the counter and said, "Let's measure you, dear." She put the tape measure all the way around me and smiled at my mother. "Twenty-eight," she said. I felt like giving her a pinch.

Then she took out a bunch of bras and put them on the counter in front of us. My mother felt them all.

"Now dear—I suggest the Gro-Bra. It grows *with* you. You're not quite ready for a double A. Suppose you try them on and see which is most comfortable." She led us to a dressing room with a pink door that locked. My mother sat in the dressing room on a chair. I took off my dress. I wasn't wearing anything underneath but pants. I picked up the first bra and stuck my arms into the straps. I couldn't fasten it in back. My mother had to help me. She adjusted the straps and felt the front of me, "How does it feel?" she asked.

"I don't know," I said.

"Is it too tight?"

"No."

"Too loose?"

"No."

"Do you like it?"

"I guess . . ."

"Try on this one."

She got me out of the first bra and into the next one. I wondered how I'd ever learn to do it by myself. Maybe my mother would have to dress me every day.

The next bra was softer than the first. My mother explained it was made of dacron. I liked the way it felt. My mother nodded. The third one was fancy. It was lace and it made me itch. My mother said it was impractical.

The saleslady knocked on the door as I was getting back into my dress. "How did we do? Did we find something?"

My mother told her *we* did. "We'll take three of these," she said, holding up the soft bra.

When we got back to the counter who should be there but Janie Loomis and her mother.

"Oh, hi, Margaret," she said. "I'm getting some winter pajamas." Her cheeks were bright red and I saw the selection of bras on the counter in front of her.

42

"Me too," I said. "I'm getting some flannel pajamas for winter."

"Well, see you Monday," Janie said.

"Right—Monday." I was plenty glad that my mother was down at the other end of the counter paying for my bras.

7

When I got home I carried my package straight to my room. I took off my dress and put on the bra. I fastened it first around my waist, then wiggled it up to where it belonged. I threw my shoulders back and stood sideways. I didn't look any different. I took out a pair of socks and stuffed one sock into each side of the bra, to see if it really grew with me. It was too tight that way, but I liked the way it looked. Like Laura Danker. I took the socks out and put them away.

My father congratulated me at dinner. "Well, you're really growing up, Margaret. No more little girl."

"Oh, Daddy!" was all I could think of to say.

On Monday I studied the boys in my class. I had to have some names for my Boy Book before three o'clock. I picked Philip Leroy because he was the best-looking one. Also Jay Hassler because he had nice brown eyes and clean fingernails. I decided to leave it at that and explain I didn't know anybody else.

Right before the bell rang Mr. Benedict told us that he was going to ask us each to do a year-long individual project.

Everybody groaned.

Mr. Benedict held up his hands. "Now it's not as bad as it sounds, class. For one thing, it's personal—between each of you and me. I'm not going to ask what your topic is. I expect you to choose it yourself and work it up in your own way. The only thing I insist on is that it be something . . . uh . . . meaningful."

More groans.

Mr. Benedict looked crushed. "I had hoped you would find this interesting."

Poor Mr. Benedict. He was really disappointed. The way he talked to us I got the feeling we made him nervous. Nobody seemed scared of him at all and you should always be a little scared of your teacher. Sometimes he just sat at his desk and looked out at us like he couldn't believe we were really there. Of course Nancy pointed out that he *never ever* called on Laura Danker. I hadn't noticed.

As we were getting in line to go home he reminded us that on Thursday we'd have a test on the first two chapters in our social studies book. He asked us to please be prepared. Most teachers never say please.

After school we went straight to Nancy's. Before we started our official meeting we talked about Mr. Benedict and his project. We all agreed it was crazy and none of us could think of a single idea.

Then Nancy called the role. "Veronica?"

"I'm here," Gretchen said.

"Kimberly?"

"I'm here," Janie said.

"Mavis?"

"I'm here," I said.

"And so am I . . . Alexandra." Nancy closed the roll book. "Well, let's get to it. We all feel each other's backs to make sure we're wearing our bras."

We all were.

"What size did you get, Janie?" Gretchen asked.

"I got a Gro-Bra," Janie said.

"Me too," I said.

"Me too!" Gretchen laughed.

"Not me," Nancy said, proudly. "Mine's a thirty-two double A."

We were all impressed.

"If you ever want to get out of those baby bras you have to exercise," she told us.

"What kind of exercise?" Gretchen asked.

"Like this," Nancy said. She made fists, bent her arms at the elbow and moved them back and forth, sticking her chest way out. She said, "I must—I must—I must increase my bust." She said it over and over. We copied her movements and chanted with her. "We must—we must—we must increase our bust!"

"Good," Nancy told us. "Do it thirty-five times a day and I promise you'll see the results."

"Now, for our Boy Books," Gretchen said. "Is everybody ready?"

We put our Boy Books on the floor and Nancy picked them up, one at a time. She read each one and passed it around for the rest of us to see. Janie's was first. She had seven names listed. Number one was Philip Leroy. Gretchen had four names. Number one was Philip Leroy. Nancy listed eighteen boys. I didn't even know eighteen boys! And number one was Philip Leroy. When Nancy got to my Boy Book she choked on an ice cube from her glass of coke. When she stopped choking she read, "Number one—Philip Leroy." Everybody giggled. "Number two—Jay Hassler. How come you picked him?"

I was getting mad. I mean, she didn't ask the others why they liked this one or that one, so why should I have to tell? I raised my eyebrow at Nancy, then looked away. She got the message.

When we were through, Nancy opened her bedroom door. There were Evan and Moose, eavesdropping. They followed us down the stairs and outside. When Nancy said, "Get lost, we're busy," Evan and Moose burst out laughing.

They shouted, "We must—we must—we must increase our bust!" Then they fell on the grass and rolled over and over laughing so hard I hoped they would both wet their pants.

On Wednesday, during an arithmetic review, I heard a bird go *peep*. Lots of other kids heard it too and so did Mr. Benedict. I know because he looked up. I went back to my problems but pretty soon I heard it again. *Peep*.

After the second *peep*, Mr. Benedict walked to the window and opened it wide. He stuck his head way out looking all around. While he was doing that three more *peeps* came from the room. Mr. Benedict walked to his desk and stood with his hands behind his back. *Peep*. I looked at Nancy. I was sure it came from her. But she didn't look at me or say anything. Mr. Benedict sat down and tapped his fingers on the top of his desk. Pretty soon our room sounded like a pet store full of birds. Every second there was another *peep*. It was hard not to giggle. When Nancy kicked me under the table I knew it was my turn. I looked down and erased my answer to a problem. While I was blowing the eraser dust away I said it—*peep*. By the time Mr. Benedict looked my way another *peep* came from across the room. I think it was Philip Leroy. We kept waiting for Mr. Benedict to say something, but he didn't.

When we came in the next morning our desks had been rearranged. Instead of four tables our desks formed one big U shape across the room. There were name cards taped onto each desk. On one side I was next to Freddy Barnett, who I didn't like at all. I knew for a fact that he was a troublemaker because I saw him stand behind Jay Hassler on the first day of school and just as Jay was about to sit down, Freddy

Barnett pulled his chair away. Jay wound up on the floor. I hate kids who do that! I'd have to be very careful not to fall into the trap of the Lobster. That's what we call him because on the first day of school he was sunburned bright red.

But on the other side of me things were even worse. I was next to Laura Danker! I was afraid to even look her way. Nancy warned me that reputations were catching. Well, I didn't have to worry because Laura didn't look my way either. She looked straight ahead. Naturally, the Four PTS's were all separated. But Nancy (that lucky!) got to sit next to Philip Leroy!

There wasn't any more *peep*ing. Mr. Benedict reminded us of our social studies test the next day. That afternoon we had gym. The boys got to play baseball with Mr. Benedict. The girls were left with the gym teacher, Miss Abbott, who told us to line up in order of size. I was third from the front end. Janie was first. Laura Danker was last. Gretchen and Nancy were in the middle. After we lined up Miss Abbott talked about posture and how important it is to stand up straight. "No matter how tall you are you must never slouch, because height is such a blessing. With that Miss Abbott stood up and took some deep breaths. She must have been at least six feet tall. Janie and I looked at each other and giggled. We were not blessed.

Then Miss Abbott told us since we were in sixth grade and very grown up, there were certain subjects we would cover during the school year. "Certain very private subjects just for girls." That was all she said but I got the idea. Why do they wait until sixth grade when you already know everything!

That night I really worked hard. I read the first two chapters in my social studies book four times. Then I sat on my bedroom floor and did my exercise. "I must—I must—I must increase my bust!" I did it thirty-five times and climbed into bed.

Are you there God? It's me, Margaret. I just did an exercise to help me grow. Have you thought about it God? About my growing, I mean. I've got a bra now. It would be nice if I had something to put in it. Of course, if you don't think I'm ready I'll understand. I'm having a test in school tomorrow. Please let me get a good grade on it God. I want you to be proud of me. Thank you.

The next morning Mr. Benedict passed out the test paper himself. The questions were already on the board. He said to begin as soon as we got our paper. Freddy the Lobster poked me and whispered, "No name."

"What do you mean, no name?" I whispered back.

Freddy whispered, "Nobody signs his name. Benedict won't know whose paper is whose. Get it?"

I got it all right but I didn't like it. Especially since I'd read the chapters four times. But if nobody was going to put a name on the test paper, I wasn't going to either. I felt cheated because Mr. Benedict would never know how hard I'd studied.

I answered all the questions in fifteen minutes. Mr. Benedict asked Janie to collect the papers for him. I couldn't imagine what he would do to us when he found out nobody had put a name on the test. I figured he'd be plenty mad but you can't do much to a whole class except keep them after school. We couldn't all be expelled, could we?

8

On Friday morning when we walked into our room, there was a test paper on everyone's desk. Every paper was marked and had the proper name on it. I got a ninety-eight. I felt great. Freddy Barnett didn't feel great at all. He got a fifty-three! Mr. Benedict didn't say anything about our names not being on the test papers. He just stood there and smiled. "Good morning, class," he said without clearing his throat. I think he knew he'd won the battle.

Later that day Mr. Benedict reminded us of our individual projects again. He told us not to wait until the last minute and think we could whip something up then. He said by the end of next week we should all know our topic and start in on our notes.

I thought a lot about it, but I didn't know anything meaningful that I was willing to share with Mr. Benedict. I mean, I couldn't very well come up with a year-long study about bras and what goes in them. Or about my feelings toward Moose. Or about God. Or could I? I mean, not about God exactly—I could never tell Mr. Benedict that—but maybe about religion. If I could figure out which religion to be I'd know if I wanted to join the Y or the Jewish Community Center. That was meaningful, wasn't it? I'd have to think about it.

Are you there God? It's me, Margaret. What would you think of me doing a project on religion? You wouldn't mind, would you God? I'd tell you all about it. And I won't make any decisions without asking you first. I think it's time for me to decide what to be. I can't go on being nothing forever, can I?

The following Saturday morning my mother drove me to the highway to get the New York bus. It was my first time going alone and my mother was nervous.

"Listen, Margaret—don't sit next to any men. Either sit alone or pick out a nice lady. And try to sit up front. If the bus isn't air-conditioned open your window. And when you get there ask a *lady* to show you the way downstairs. Grandma will meet you at the information desk."

"I know, I know." We'd been over it three dozen times but when the bus came my mother got out of the car and shouted to the bus driver.

"This little girl is traveling alone. Please keep an eye on her. It's her first trip."

"Don't worry, lady," the bus driver told my mother. Then my mother waved to me. I made a face at her and looked the other way.

I found grandma right where she was supposed to

be. She gave me a big kiss. Grandma smelled delicious. She was wearing a green suit and had on lots of green eyeshadow to match. Her hair was silver blonde. Grandma's hair color changes about once a month.

When we were out of the bus terminal Grandma said, "You look beautiful, Margaret. I love your hair."

Grandma always has something nice to say to me. And my hair did look better. I read that if you brush it good it can grow up to an inch a month.

We went to lunch at a restaurant near Lincoln Center. During my chocolate parfait I whispered, "I'm wearing a bra. Can you tell?"

"Of course I can tell," Grandma said.

"You can?" I was really surprised. I stopped eating. "Well, how do you think it makes me look?"

"Much older," Grandma said, between sips of her coffee. I didn't know whether to believe her or not so I believed her.

Then we went to the concert. I didn't fidget like when I was a little kid. I sat very still and paid attention to the music. During intermission Grandma and I walked around outside. I love that fountain in the middle of Lincoln Center. I love it more than the concerts themselves. And I love to watch the people walk by. Once I saw a model having her picture taken by the fountain. It was freezing cold and she was wearing a summer dress. That's when I decided not to be a model. Even if I did get beautiful some day.

In the cab, on the way back to the bus terminal, I thought about Grandma being Jewish. She was the perfect person to help me start my project. So I asked her, "Can I go to temple with you sometime?"

Grandma absolutely stared at me. I never knew anyone could open her eyes so wide.

"What are you saying? Are you saying you want to be Jewish?" She held her breath.

"No. I'm saying I'd like to go to temple and see what it's all about."

"My Margaret!" Grandma threw her arms around me. I think the cab driver thought we were crazy. "I knew you were a Jewish girl at heart! I always knew it!" Grandma took out a lace hanky and dabbed her eyes.

"I'm not, Grandma," I insisted. "You know I'm not anything."

"You can say it, but I'll never believe it. Never!" She blew her nose. When she finished blowing she said, "I know what it is. You've made a lot of Jewish friends in Farbrook. Am I right?"

"No, Grandma. My friends have nothing to do with this."

"Then what? I don't understand."

"I just want to see what it's all about. So can I?" I certainly was not going to tell Grandma about Mr. Benedict.

Grandma sat back in her seat and beamed at me. "I'm thrilled! I'm going right home to call the rabbi.

You'll come with me on Rosh Hashanah." Then she stopped smiling and asked. "Does your mother know?"

I shook my head.

"Your father?"

I shook it again.

Grandma slapped her hand against her forehead. "Be sure to tell them it's not my idea! Would I be in trouble!"

"Don't worry, Grandma."

"That's ridiculous!" my mother said when I told her. "You know how Daddy and I feel about religion."

"You said I could choose when I grow up!"

"But you're not ready to choose yet, Margaret!"

"I just want to try it out," I argued. "I'm going to try church too, so don't get hysterical!"

"I am *not* hysterical! I just think it's foolish for a girl of your age to bother herself with religion."

"Can I go?" I asked.

"I'm not going to stop you," my mother said.

"Fine. Then I'll go."

On Rosh Hashanah morning, while I was still in bed, I said,

Are you there God? It's me, Margaret. I'm going to temple today—with Grandma. It's a holiday. I guess you know that. Well, my father thinks it's a mistake and my mother thinks the whole idea is crazy, but I'm going anyway. I'm sure this will help me decide what to be. I've never been inside a temple or a church. I'll look for you God.

9

I had a new suit and a small velvet hat. My mother said everyone wears new clothes for the Jewish holidays. It was hot for October and my father said he remembered it was always hot on the Jewish holidays when he was a kid. I had to wear white gloves. They made my hands sweat. By the time I got to New York the gloves were pretty dirty so I took them off and stuffed them into my pocketbook. Grandma met me at our usual spot in the bus terminal and took me in a taxi to her temple.

We got there at ten-thirty. Grandma had to show a card to an usher and then he led us to our seats which were in the fifth row in the middle. Grandma whispered to the people sitting near her that I was her granddaughter Margaret. The people looked at me and smiled. I smiled back. I was glad when the rabbi stepped out on the stage and held up his hands. While this was going on soft organ music played. I thought it sounded beautiful. The rabbi was dressed in a long black robe. He looked like a priest except he didn't have on the backwards collar that priests wear. Also, he had a little hat on his head that Grandma called a yarmulke.

The rabbi welcomed us and then started a lot of things I didn't understand. We had to stand up and sit down a lot and sometimes we all read together in English from a prayer book. I didn't understand too much of what I was reading. Other times the choir sang and the organ played. That was definitely the best part. Some of the service was in Hebrew and I was surprised to see that Grandma could recite along with the rabbi.

I looked around a lot, to see what was going on. But since I was in the fifth row there wasn't much for me to see, except the four rows in front of me. I knew it wouldn't be polite to actually turn my head and look behind me. There were two big silver bowls filled with white flowers up on the stage. They were very pretty.

At eleven-thirty the rabbi made a speech. A sermon, Grandma called it. At first I tried very hard to understand what he was talking about. But after a while I gave up and started counting different colored hats. I counted eight brown, six black, three red, a yellow and a leopard before the rabbi finished. Then we all stood up again and everyone sang a song in Hebrew that I didn't know. And that was it! I expected something else. I don't know what exactly. A feeling, maybe. But I suppose you have to go more than once to know what it's all about.

As we filed out of the aisles Grandma pulled me to one side, away from the crowd. "How would you like to meet the rabbi, Margaret?"

"I don't know," I said. I really wanted to get outside.

"Well, you're going to!" Grandma smiled at me. "I've told him all about you."

We stood in line waiting to shake hands with the rabbi. After a long time it was our turn. I was face to face with Rabbi Kellerman. He was kind of young and looked a little like Miles J. Benedict Jr. He wasn't skinny though.

Grandma whispered to me, "Shake hands, Margaret."

I held out my hand.

"This is my granddaughter, Rabbi. The one I told you about . . . Margaret Simon."

The rabbi shook my hand. "Yes, of course. Margaret! Good Yom Tov."

"Yes," I said.

The rabbi laughed. "It means Happy New Year. That's what we're celebrating today."

"Oh," I said. "Well, Happy New Year to you Rabbi."

"Did you enjoy our service?" he asked.

"Oh, yes," I said. "I just loved it."

"Good—good." He pumped my hand up and down some more. "Come back any time. Get to know us, Margaret. Get to know us and God."

I had to go through the third degree when I got home.

"Well," my mother said. "How was it?"

"Okay, I guess."

"Did you like it?" she asked.

"It was interesting," I said.

"Did you learn anything?" my father wanted to know.

"Well," I said. "In the first five rows there were eight brown hats and six black ones."

My father laughed. "When I was a kid I used to count feathers on hats." Then we laughed together.

Are you there God? It's me, Margaret. I'm really on my way now. By the end of the school year I'll know all there is to know about religion. And before I start junior high I'll know which one I am. Then I'll be able to join the Y or the Center like everybody else.

10

Three things happened the first week in November. Laura Danker wore a sweater to school for the first time. Mr. Benedict's eyes almost popped out of his head. Actually, I didn't notice Mr. Benedict's eyes, but Nancy told me. Freddy the Lobster noticed too. He asked me, "How come you don't look like that in a sweater, Margaret?" Then he laughed hard and slapped his leg. Very funny, I thought. I wore sweaters every day since I had so many of them. All *made expressly* for me by Grandma. Even if I stuffed my bra with socks I still wouldn't look like Laura Danker. I wondered if it was true that she went behind the A&P with Evan and Moose. Why would she do a stupid thing like that?

What reminded me of Moose was that he cut our grass and cleaned up our leaves and said he'd be back in the spring. So unless I bumped into him at Nancy's house I wouldn't see him all winter. Not that he even knew I existed—I'd had to hide from him ever since that *We must—we must* incident. But I watched him secretly from my bedroom window.

The second thing that happened was that I went to church with Janie Loomis. Janie and I had gotten pretty friendly. We were especially friendly in gym because Ruth, the girl who was second in line, was absent a lot. So Janie and I got to talk and once I came right out and asked her if she went to church.

"When I have to," she said.

So I asked her if I could go with her some time just to see what it was like and she said, "Sure, how about Sunday?"

So I went. The funniest thing was it was just like temple. Except it was all in English. But we read from a prayer book that didn't make sense and the minister gave a sermon I couldn't follow and I counted eight black hats, four red ones, six blue and two fur. At the end of the service everyone sang a hymn. Then we stood on line to shake hands with the minister. By then I was a pro at it.

Janie introduced me. "This is my friend Margaret Simon. She's no religion."

I almost fainted. What did Janie have to go and say that for? The minister looked at me like I was a freak. Then he smiled with an Aha—maybe-I'll-win-her look.

"Welcome to the First Presbyterian Church, Margaret. I hope you'll come back again."

"Thank you," I said.

Are you there God? It's me, Margaret. I've been to church. I didn't feel anything special in there God. Even though I wanted to. I'm sure it has nothing to do with you. Next time I'll try harder.

During this time I talked to Nancy every night. My father wanted to know why we had to phone each other so often when we were together in school all day. "What can you possibly have to discuss after only three hours?" he asked. I didn't even try to explain. Lots of times we did our math homework over the phone. When we were done Nancy called Gretchen to check answers and I called Janie.

The third thing that happened that week was the principal of our school announced over the loudspeaker that the PTA was giving a Thanksgiving square dance for the three sixth-grade classes. Mr. Benedict asked us if we knew how to square dance. Most of us didn't.

Nancy told the Four PTS's the square dance was going to be really super. And she knew all about it because her mother was on the committee. She said we should all write down who we wanted to dance with and she'd see what she could do about it. It turned out that we all wanted Philip Leroy, so Nancy said, "Forget it—I'm no magician."

For the next two weeks our gym period was devoted to square-dancing lessons. Mr. Benedict said if we were being given this party the least we could do to show our appreciation was to learn to do the basic steps. We practiced with records and Mr. Benedict jumped around a lot, clapping his hands. When he had to demonstrate a step he used Laura Danker as his partner. He said it was because she was tall enough to reach his shoulder properly, but Nancy gave me a knowing look. Anyway, none of the boys in our class wanted to be Laura's partner because they were all a lot smaller than her. Even Philip Leroy only came up to her chin, and he was the tallest.

The problem with square-dance lessons was that most of the boys were a lot more interested in stepping on our feet than they were in learning how to dance. And a few of them were so good at it they could step on us in time to the music. Mostly, I concentrated on not getting my feet squashed.

On the morning of the square dance I dressed in my new skirt and blouse.

Are you there God? It's me, Margaret. I can't wait until two o'clock God. That's when our dance starts. Do you think I'll get Philip Leroy for a partner? It's not so much that I like him as a person God, but as a boy he's very handsome. And I'd love to dance with him . . . just once or twice. Thank you God.

The PTA decorated the gym. It was supposed to look like a barn, I think. There were two piles of hay and three scarecrows. And a big sign on the wall in yellow letters saying WELCOME TO THE SIXTH GRADE SQUARE DANCE . . . as if we didn't know.

I was glad my mother wasn't a chaperone. It's bad enough trying to act natural at a dance, but when

65

your mother's there it's impossible. I know because Mrs. Wheeler was a chaperone and Nancy was a wreck. The chaperones were dressed funny, like farmers or something. I mean, Nancy's mother wore dungarees, a plaid shirt and a big straw hat. I didn't blame Nancy for pretending not to know her.

We had a genuine square-dance caller. He was dressed up a lot like Mrs. Wheeler. He stood on the stage and told us what steps to do. He also worked the record player. He stamped his feet and jumped around and now and then I saw him mop his face off with a red handkerchief. Mr. Benedict kept telling us to get into the spirit of the party. "Relax and enjoy yourselves," he said.

The three sixth grades were supposed to mingle but the Four PTS's stuck close together. We had to line up every time there was a new dance. The girls lined up on one side and the boys on the other. That's how you got a partner. The only trouble was there were four more girls than boys, so whoever wound up last on line had to dance with another leftover girl. That only happened to me and Janie once, thank goodness!

What we did was try to figure out who our partner was going to be in advance. Like, I knew when I was fourth in line that Norman Fishbein was going to be my partner because he was fourth in line on the boys' side. So I switched around fast because Norman Fishbein is the biggest drip in my class. Well, at least one of the biggest drips. Also, Freddy Barnett was to be avoided because all he would do was tease me about how come I didn't look like Laura Danker in a sweater. But I noticed that once when he danced with her his face was so red he looked more like a lobster than he did when he was all sunburned.

The girls shuffled around more than the boys because most of us wanted to get Philip Leroy for a partner. And finally I got him. This is how it happened. After everyone had a partner we had to make a square. My partner was Jay Hassler who was very polite and didn't try to step on my foot once. Then the caller told us to switch partners with whoever was on our right side. Well, Philip Leroy was with Nancy on my right side, and Nancy was so mad she almost cried right in front of everyone. Even though I was thrilled to have Philip Leroy all to myself for a whole record, he *was* one of the foot steppers! And dancing with him made my hands sweat so bad I had to wipe them off on my new skirt.

At four o'clock the chaperones served us punch and cookies and at quarter to five the dance was over and my mother picked me up in our new car. (My father gave in around Halloween when my mother explained that she couldn't even get a quart of milk because she had no car. And that *Margaret* couldn't possibly walk to and from school in bad weather and that bad weather would be coming very soon. My mother didn't like my father's suggestion that if she got up early and drove him to the station she could use his car all day long.) Our new car is a Chevy. It's green.

My mother was in a hurry to drive home from the square dance because she was in the middle of a new painting. It was a picture of a lot of different fruits in honor of Thanksgiving. My mother gives away a whole bunch of pictures every Christmas. My father thinks they wind up in other people's attics.

11

By the first week in December we no longer used our secret names at PTS meetings. It was too confusing, Nancy said. Also, we just about gave up on our Boy Books. For one thing the names never changed. Nancy managed to shift hers around. It was easy for her—with eighteen boys. But Janie and Gretchen and I always listed Philip Leroy number one. There was no suspense about the whole thing. And I wondered, did they list Philip Leroy because they really liked him or were they doing what I did—making him number one because he was so good-looking. Maybe they were ashamed to write who they really liked too.

The day that Gretchen finally got up the guts to sneak out her father's anatomy book we met at my house, in my bedroom, with the door closed and a chair shoved in front of it. We sat on the floor in a circle with the book opened to the male body.

"Do you suppose that's what Philip Leroy looks like without his clothes on?" Janie asked.

"Naturally, dope!" Nancy said. "He's male, isn't he?"

"Look at all those veins and stuff," Janie said.

"Well, we *all* have them," Gretchen said.

69

"I think they're ugly," Janie said.

"You better never be a doctor or a nurse," Gretchen told her. "They have to look at this stuff all the time."

"Turn the page, Gretchen," Nancy said.

The next page was the male reproductive system. None of us said anything. We just looked until Nancy told us, "My brother looks like that."

"How do you know?" I asked.

"He walks around naked," Nancy said.

"My father used to walk around naked," Gretchen said. "But lately he's stopped doing it."

"My aunt went to a nudist colony last summer," Janie said.

"No kidding!" Nancy looked up.

"She stayed a month," Janie told us. "My mother didn't talk to her for three weeks after that. She thought it was a disgrace. My aunt's divorced."

"Because of the nudist colony?" I asked.

"No," Janie said. "She was divorced before she went."

"What do you suppose they do there?" Gretchen asked.

"Just walk around naked is all. My aunt says it's very peaceful. But I'll never walk around naked in front of anybody!"

"What about when you get married?" Gretchen asked.

"Even then," Janie insisted.

"You're a prude!" Nancy said.

"I am not! It has nothing to do with being a prude."

"When you grow you'll change your mind," Nancy told her. "You'll want everybody to see you. Like those girls in *Playboy*."

"What girls in *Playboy?*" Janie asked.

"Didn't you *ever* see a copy of *Playboy?*"

"Where would I see it?" Janie asked.

"My father gets it," I said.

"Do you have it around?" Nancy asked.

"Sure."

"Well, get it!" Nancy told me.

"Now?" I asked.

"Of course."

"Well, I don't know," I said.

"Listen, Margaret—Gretchen went to all the trouble of sneaking out her father's medical book. The least you could do is show us *Playboy*."

So I opened my bedroom door and went downstairs, trying to remember where I had seen the latest issue. I didn't want to ask my mother. Not that it was so wrong to show it to my friends. I mean, if it was so wrong my father shouldn't get it at all, right? Although lately I think he's been hiding it because it's never in the magazine rack where it used to be. Finally, I found it in his night table drawer and I thought if my mother caught me and asked me what I was doing I'd say we were making booklets and I needed some old magazines to cut up. But she didn't catch me.

Nancy opened it right up to the naked girl in the

middle. On the page before there was a story about her. It said Hillary Brite is eighteen years old.

"Eighteen! That's only six more years," Nancy squealed.

"But look at the size of her. They're huge!" Janie said.

"Do you suppose we'll look like that at eighteen?" Gretchen asked.

"If you ask me, I think there's something wrong with her," I said. "She looks out of proportion!"

"Do you suppose that's what Laura Danker looks like?" Janie asked.

"No. Not yet," Nancy said. "But she might at eighteen!"

Our meeting ended with fifty rounds of "*We must —we must—we must increase our bust!*"

12

On December eleventh Grandma sailed on a three-week cruise to the Caribbean. She went every year. She had a bon voyage party in her room on the ship. This year I was allowed to go. My mother gave Grandma a green silk box to keep her jewelry safe. It was very nice—all lined in white velvet. Grandma said thank you and that all her jewelry was for "her Margaret" anyway so she had to take good care of it. Grandma's always reminding me of how nobody lives forever and everything she has is for me and I hate it when she talks like that. She once told me she had her lawyer prepare her funeral instructions so things would go the way she planned. Such as, the kind of box she wants to be buried in and that she doesn't want any speeches at all and that I should only come once or twice a year to see that her grave is looking nice and neat.

We stayed on the ship half an hour and then Grandma kissed me good-by and promised to take me along with her one of these days.

The next week my mother started to address her Christmas cards and for days at a time she was frantically busy with them. She doesn't call them Christmas cards. Holiday greetings, she says. We don't celebrate

Christmas exactly. We give presents but my parents say that's a traditional American custom. My father says my mother and her greeting cards have to do with her childhood. She sends them to people she grew up with and they send cards back to her. So once a year she finds out who married whom and who had what kids and stuff like that. Also, she sends one to her brother, whom I've never met. He lives in California.

This year I discovered something really strange. I discovered that my mother was sending a Christmas card to her parents in Ohio. I found out because I was looking through the pile of cards one day when I had a cold and stayed home from school. There it was—just like that. The envelope said Mr. and Mrs. Paul Hutchins, and that's them. My grandparents! I didn't mention anything about it to my mother. I had the feeling I wasn't supposed to know.

In school, Mr. Benedict was running around trying to find out what happened to the new choir robes. The whole school was putting on a Christmas–Hanukkah pageant for the parents and our sixth-grade class was the choir. We didn't even have to try out. "Mr. Benedict's class will be the choir," the principal announced. We practiced singing every day with the music teacher. I thought by the time Christmas finally rolled around I wouldn't have any voice left. We learned five Christmas carols and three Hanukkah songs—alto and soprano parts. Mostly the boys sang alto and the girls sang soprano. We'd been measured for our new choir robes right after Thanksgiving. The PTA decided the old ones were really worn out. Our new ones would be green instead of black. We all had to carry pencil-sized flashlights instead of candles.

We practiced marching down the halls and into the auditorium singing "*Adeste Fidelis*" in English and Latin. We marched in two lines, boys and girls. And naturally in size places. I walked right behind Janie because Ruth had moved away. My partner turned out to be Norman Fishbein. I never looked at him. I just marched looking straight ahead singing very loud.

A week before the pageant Alan Gordon told Mr. Benedict that he wasn't going to sing the Christmas songs because it was against his religion. Then Lisa Murphy raised her hand and said that she wasn't going to sing the Hanukkah songs because it was against *her* religion.

Mr. Bendict explained that songs were for everyone and had nothing at all to do with religion, but the next day Alan brought in a note from home and from then on he marched but he didn't sing. Lisa sang when we marched but she didn't even move her lips during the Hanukkah songs.

Are you there God? It's me, Margaret. I want you to know I'm giving a lot of thought to Christmas

75

and Hanukkah this year. I'm trying to decide if one might be special for me. I'm really thinking hard God. But so far I haven't come up with any answers.

Our new green choir robes were delivered to school the day before the pageant and were sent home with us to be pressed. The best thing about the pageant, besides wearing the robe and carrying the flashlight, was that I got to sit in the first row of choir seats, facing the audience, which meant that the kindergarten kids were right in front of me. Some of them tried to touch our feet with their feet. One little kid wet his pants during the scene where Mary and Joseph come to the inn. He made a puddle on the floor right in front of Janie. Janie had to keep on singing and pretend she didn't know. It was pretty hard not to laugh.

School closed for vacation right after the pageant. When I got home my mother told me I had a letter.

13

"Margaret—you've got a letter," my mother called from the studio. "It's on the front table."

I just about never get any letters. Probably because I never write anybody back. So I dashed over to the front table and picked it up. *Miss Margaret Simon*, it said. I turned the envelope around but there was no return address. I wondered who sent it. Wondering made it much more fun than ripping it open and knowing right away. It was probably just an advertisement anyway. Finally, when I couldn't stand it any more I opened it—very slowly and *very* carefully so I wouldn't rip up the envelope. It was an invitation! I knew right away because of the picture—a bunch of kids dancing around a record. Also, it said, HAVING A PARTY.

Who's having a party, I thought. Who's having a party and invited me? Naturally I could have found out right away. I could have looked inside. But this was better. I considered the possibilities. It couldn't be a PTS because I would have known. It could be somebody I knew from New York or camp, except I hadn't written to any old friends to tell them my new address.

Anyway, the envelope was postmarked New Jersey. Let's see, I thought. Who could it be? Who? Finally, I opened it.

Come on over on Satı'rday, Dec. 20
from 5 PM *to 9* PM *(supper)*
1334 Whittingham Terrace
Norman Fishbein

"Norman Fishbein!" I yelled. That drip! I never even talked to him. Why would he invite me to his party? Still, a party is a party. And for supper too!

"Hey Mom!" I yelled, running into the studio. My mother was standing away from her canvas, studying her work. Her paint brush was in her mouth, between her teeth. "Guess what, Mom?"

"What?" she said, not taking the paint brush away.

"I'm invited to a supper party. Here—look—" I showed her my invitation.

She read it. "Who's Norman Fishbein?" She took the paint brush out of her mouth.

"A kid in my class."

"Do you like him?"

"He's okay. Can I go?"

"Well . . . I suppose so." My mother dabbed some red paint on her canvas. Then the phone rang.

"I'll get it." I ran into the kitchen and said a breathless hello.

78

"It's Nancy. Did you get invited?"

"Yes," I said. "Did you?"

"Mmm. We all did. Janie and Gretchen too."

"Can you go?"

"Sure."

"Me too."

"I've never been to a supper party," Nancy said.

"Me either. Should we dress up?" I asked.

"My mother's going to call Mrs. Fishbein. I'll let you know." She hung up.

Ten minutes later the phone rang again. I answered.

"Margaret. It's me again."

"I know."

"You'll never believe this!" Nancy said.

"What? What won't I believe?"

"We're all invited."

"What do you mean *all?*"

"Our whole class."

"All twenty-eight of us?"

"That's what Mrs. Fishbein told my mother."

"Even Laura?"

"I guess so."

"Do you think she'll come?" I asked, trying to picture Laura at a party.

"Well, her mother and Mrs. Fishbein work on a lot of committees together. So maybe her mother will make her."

"How about Philip Leroy?"

"He's invited. That's all I know. And Mrs. Fishbein said definitely party clothes."

When I hung up I raced back to the studio. "Mom —our whole class is invited!"

"Your *whole* class?" My mother put her paint brush down and looked at me.

"Yes. All twenty-eight of us."

"Mrs. Fishbein must be crazy!" my mother said.

"Should I wear my velvet, do you think?"

"It's your best. You might as well."

On the day of the party I talked to Nancy six times, to Janie three times and to Gretchen twice. Nancy called me back every time she changed her mind about what to wear. And each time she asked me if I was still wearing my velvet. I told her I was. The rest of the time we made our arrangements. We decided that Nancy would sleep over at my house and that Gretchen would sleep over at Janie's. Mr. Wheeler would drive us all to the party and Mr. Loomis would drive us home.

My mother washed my hair at two o'clock. She gave me a cream rinse too, so I wouldn't get tangles. She set it in big rollers all over my head. I sat under her hair dryer. Then she *filed* my nails with an emery board instead of just cutting them like usual. My velvet dress was already laid out on my bed along with my new underwear, party shoes and tights. My new under-wear was not the ordinary cotton kind. It was nylon, trimmed with lace around the edges. It was supposed to be one of my December tradition gifts. All afternoon I kept thinking that maybe Norman Fishbein wasn't such a drip.

After my bath I was supposed to go to my room and rest so I'd be in good shape for the party. I went to my room and closed the door—only I didn't feel like resting. What I did was move my desk chair in front of my dresser mirror. Then I stood on the chair and took off my robe. I stood naked in front of the mirror. I was starting to get some hairs. I turned around and studied myself sideways. Then I got off the chair and moved it closer to the mirror. I stood back up on it and looked again. My head looked funny with all those rollers. The rest of me looked the same.

Are you there God? It's me, Margaret. I hate to remind you God . . . I mean, I know you're busy. But it's already December and I'm not growing. At least I don't see any real difference. Isn't it time God? Don't you think I've waited patiently? Please help me.

I hopped off the chair and sat down on the edge of my bed, putting on my clean underwear and tights. Then I stood in front of the mirror again. I didn't look at myself for very long this time.

I went into the bathroom and opened the bottom cabinet. There was a whole box of cotton balls. *Sterile until opened*, the package said. I reached in and grabbed a few. My heart was pounding, which seemed stupid because what was I so afraid of anyway? I mean, if my mother saw me grab some cotton balls she wouldn't say anything. I use them all the time—to put calamine on my summer mosquito bites—to clean off cuts and bruises—to put on my face lotion at night. But my heart kept pounding anyway, because I knew what I was going to do with the cotton balls.

I tiptoed back to my room and closed the door. I stepped into my closet and stood in one corner. I shoved three cotton balls into each side of my bra. Well, so what if it was cheating! Probably other girls did it too. I'd look a lot better, wouldn't I? So why not!

I came out of the closet and got back up on my chair. This time when I turned sideways I looked like I'd grown. I liked it!

Are you still there God? See how nice my bra looks now! That's all I need—just a little help. I'll really be good around the house God. I'll clear the table every night for a month at least! Please God . . .

14

Later, my mother brushed my hair. It came out just right, except for one piece on the left that turned the wrong way. My mother said that piece made it look very natural.

My mother and father smiled at me a lot while I was waiting for Nancy's father to pick me up. I smiled back. It was like we all knew some special secret. Only I knew they didn't know *my* special secret! At least they didn't say anything dumb like doesn't she look sweet—going to her first supper party! I'd have died!

Mr. Wheeler tooted his horn at quarter to five. My mother kissed me good-by and my father waved from his chair. "Have fun," he called.

The Four PTS's squeezed into the back seat of the Wheeler car (not the station wagon). Nancy's father told us it was silly to sit like that and besides it made him feel like a hired chauffeur. But all we did was giggle. Janie got her hair cut without telling us she was going to. She said she didn't know it herself until that afternoon when her mother took her to the beauty parlor and had a private talk with Mr. Anthony. Then Mr. Anthony started clipping away and next thing she knew—she had this new haircut. She looked like an elf. It did a lot for her. And for a minute I thought about how I would look with the same haircut. But then I remembered how long I'd been suffering to let my hair grow. I decided it would be stupid to cut it all off.

When we got to the party Norman's mother opened the door for us. She was very tall and thin with a face like Norman's. I remembered her from the PTA square dance. Tonight she wasn't dressed like a farmer. She had on black velvet pants and some kind of top that looked like it had diamonds and rubies all over it.

"Good evening, Mrs. Fishbein," Nancy said, in a voice I'd never heard. "Please meet my friend Margaret Simon."

Mrs. Fishbein smiled at me and said, "Glad to meet you, Margaret." Then she took our coats away and handed them to a maid who carried them up the stairs.

"My, you all look so pretty!" Mrs. Fishbein said. "Everyone is downstairs. Nancy, you know the way."

I followed Nancy past the living room. The furniture was all very modern. The chairs looked like carved-out boxes and the tables were all glass. Everything was beige. At Nancy's house the furniture all has lion's paws for feet and there are a million colors. At my house the living room is carpeted but empty. My mother is trying to decide what kind of stuff she wants.

Noman's house was pretty big, because I had to follow Nancy through at least four more rooms before we got to a door leading downstairs.

It looked like most of my class was already there. Including Laura Danker, who I thought looked gorgeous in a soft pink dress with her hair all loose, kind of hanging in her face.

The boys had on sport jackets and some wore ties. Philip Leroy had on a tie the first time I saw him but a few minutes later the tie was gone and his shirt was unbuttoned around the neck. Soon after that, not one boy had his jacket on. They were all in a big heap in the corner.

Mostly, the girls stayed on one side of the room, and the boys on the other. As soon as everyone was there Mrs. Fishbein brought out the food. All kinds of sandwiches and a big dish of cut-up hotdogs in beans. I took some of that and some potato salad and sat down at a table with Janie, Nancy and Gretchen. There were six little tables so practically everyone had a place to sit. As soon as we were all served Mrs. Fishbein and the maid went back upstairs.

I'm not sure who started blowing the mustard through a straw up at the ceiling. I only know that I saw Philip Leroy yell, "Watch this, Freddy!" as he aimed his straw. I saw the mustard fly up and make a yellow splotch on the white ceiling.

Mrs. Fishbein didn't come downstairs again until dessert time. At first she didn't see the ceiling. But she did see the mess on the buffet table. When she looked up she sucked in her breath and the room got very quiet. "What is that on my ceiling?" she asked Norman.

"Mustard," Norman answered.

"I see," Mrs. Fishbein replied.

That was all she said but she looked at every one of us with an I-don't-know-why-your-parents-never-taught-you-any-manners look. Then Mrs. Fishbein stood close to our table and said, "I'm sure these girls aren't responsible for this mess." We smiled at her, but I saw Philip Leroy stick out his tongue at us.

"Now I'm going upstairs to get your dessert," Mrs. Fishbein said, "and I expect you to behave like ladies and gentlemen."

Dessert was tiny cupcakes in all different colors. I ate two chocolate ones before Freddy Barnett came over to our table. "I'm sure these girls didn't do anything naughty!" he mimicked. "These girls are so sweet and good."

"Oh shut up!" Nancy told him, standing up. She was as tall as he was.

"Why don't you shut up, *know it all!*"

"Cut it out, Lobster!" Nancy hollered.

"Who's a lobster?"

"You are!" Nancy gritted her teeth.

Freddy grabbed hold of Nancy and for a minute I thought he was going to hit her.

"Take you lobster claws off me!" Nancy yelled.

"Make me," Freddy told her.

Nancy whirled around but Freddy had hold of her dress by the pocket and next thing we knew Freddy still had the pocket but Nancy was across the room.

"Oh! He ripped off my pocket!" Nancy screamed.

Freddy looked like he couldn't believe it himself. But there he was, holding Nancy's pocket. There wasn't any hole in Nancy's dress—just some loose threads where her pocket used to be. Nancy ran up the stairs and returned a few minutes later with Mrs. Fishbein.

"He tore off my pocket," Nancy said, pointing to Freddy Barnett.

"I didn't mean to," Freddy explained. "It just came off."

"I am shocked at your behavior. *Simply shocked!*" Mrs. Fishbein said. "I don't know what kind of children you are. I'm not going to send you home because your parents expect you to be here until nine and it's only seven now. But I'm telling you this—any more hanky-panky and I'll call each and every one of your mothers and fathers and report this *abominable* behavior to them!"

Mrs. Fishbein marched back up the stairs. We couldn't hold back our giggles. It was all so funny. *Hanky-panky* and *abominable!*

Even Nancy and Freddy had to laugh. Then Norman suggested that we play games to keep out of trouble. "The first game is Guess Who," Norman said.

"Guess Who?" Janie asked. "How do you play that?"

Norman explained. "See, I turn off all the lights and the boys line up on one side and the girls on the other and then when I yell Go the boys run to the girls' side and try to guess who's who by the way they feel."

"No, thank you," Gretchen said. "That's disgusting!"

"Above the neck, Gretchen," Norman said. "Only above the neck."

"Forget it," Gretchen said and we all agreed. Especially me—I kept thinking of those six cotton balls. They weren't so far below my neck.

"Okay," Norman said. "We'll start with Spin the Bottle."

"That's corny!" Philip Leroy shouted.

"Yeah," the other boys agreed.

"We have to start with something," Norman said. He put a green bottle on the floor.

We sat in a big circle, around the green bottle. Norman told us his rules. "You got to kiss whoever's nearest to where the bottle points. No fair boy kissing boy or girl kissing girl."

Norman spun first. He got Janie. He bent down and gave her a kiss on the cheek, near her ear but up higher. He ran back to his place in the circle. Everybody laughed. Then Janie had to spin. She got Jay. She put her face next to his but she kissed the air instead of him.

88

"No fair!" Norman called out. "You've got to *really* kiss him."

"Okay, okay," Janie said. She tried again. She made it this time, but far away from his mouth.

I felt a lot safer knowing it would all be cheek kissing. I held my breath every time somebody turned the bottle, waiting to see who would get me and wondering who I would get. When Gretchen got Philip Leroy she could hardly stand up. She kept biting her lip and finally she went over to him and gave him the quickest kiss you ever saw. Then I really couldn't breathe because I thought, if he gets me I'll faint. I closed my eyes. When I opened them I saw the bottle pointing straight at Laura Danker. She looked down and when Philip bent to kiss her I think all he got was her forehead and some loose hair.

That's when Jay said, "This is *really* stupid. Let's play Two Minutes in the Closet."

"What's that?" Norman asked.

Jay explained. "We all get a number and then somebody starts by calling like—number six—and those two go in the closet for two minutes and uh . . . well, you know."

"We don't have a closet down here," Norman said. "But we do have a bathroom."

Norman didn't waste any time getting some paper and pencils. He scribbled the numbers on a big sheet of paper—odd ones for the boys, evens for the girls. Then he tore each number off and put first the evens, then the odds in his father's hat. We all picked. I got number twelve.

I was half scared and half excited and I wished I had been experimenting like Nancy. Nancy would know what to do with a boy in the dark, but what did I know? Nothing!

Norman said he'd go first because it was his party. Nobody argued. He stood up and cleared his throat. "Number uh . . . number sixteen," he said.

Gretchen squealed and jumped up.

"Bye bye you two," Nancy said. "Don't be long!"

Long! They were back in three seconds.

"Hey! I thought you said two minutes," Philip Leroy called.

"Two minutes is as long as you can stay," Norman said. "But you don't have to stay that long if you don't want to."

Gretchen called number three which was Freddy Barnett and I hoped I'd remember to never call number three.

Then Freddy called number fourteen and got Laura Danker. We all giggled. I wondered how he would kiss her because I didn't think he could reach her face unless he stood on something. Maybe he'll stand on the toilet seat, I thought. And then I couldn't stop laughing at all.

When they came out of the bathroom Laura's face was as red as Freddy's and I thought that was pretty funny for a girl who goes behind the A&P with boys.

Laura called her number very softly. "Seven," she said.

Philip Leroy stood up and smiled at the boys. He pushed his hair off his face and walked to the bathroom with his hands stuffed in his pockets. I kept thinking that if he really liked her he'd call her number back and the two of them would be in the bathroom together for the rest of the party.

When they came out Philip was still smiling but Laura wasn't. Nancy poked me and gave me her knowing look. I was so busy watching Laura that I didn't hear Philip call number twelve.

"Who's twelve?" Philip asked. "Somebody must be twelve."

"Did you say twelve?" I asked. "That's me."

"Well, come on, Margaret."

I stood up knowing I'd never be able to make it across the recreation room to the bathroom, where Philip Leroy was waiting to kiss me. I saw Janie, Gretchen and Nancy smiling at me. But I couldn't smile back. I don't know how I got to the bathroom. All I know is I stepped in and Philip shut the door. It was hard to see anything.

"Hi, Margaret," he said.

"Hi, Philip," I whispered. Then I started to giggle.

"I can't kiss you if you don't stop laughing," he said.

"Why not?"

"Because your mouth is open when you laugh."

"You're going to kiss me on the mouth?"

"You know a better place?"

I stopped laughing. I wished I could remember what Nancy said that day she showed me how to kiss her pillow.

"Stand still, Margaret," Philip told me.

I stood still.

He put his hands on my shoulders and leaned close. Then he kissed me. A really fast kiss! Not the kind you see in the movies where the boy and girl cling together for a long time. While I was thinking about it, Philip kissed me again. Then he opened the bathroom door and walked back to his place.

"Call a number, Margaret," Norman said. "Hurry up."

I couldn't even think of a number. I wanted to call Philip Leroy's number. But I couldn't remember it. So I called number nine and got Norman Fishbein!

He was really proud. Like I'd picked him on purpose. Ha! He practically ran to the bathroom.

After he closed the door he said, "I really like you, Margaret. How do you want me to kiss you?"

"On the cheek and fast," I said.

He did it just that way and I quickly opened the door and walked away from the bathroom. And that was it!

Later, at my house, Nancy told me she thought I was the luckiest girl in the world and maybe it was fate that brought me and Philip Leroy together.

"Did he kiss good?" she asked.
"Pretty good," I said.
"How many times?" she asked.
"About five. I lost count," I told her.
"Did he *say* anything?"
"Nothing much."
"Do you still like him?"
"Of course!"
"Me too."
"Good night, Nancy."
"Good night, Margaret."

15

I went to Christmas Eve services with the Wheelers, at the United Methodist Church of Farbrook. I asked Nancy if I had to meet the minister.

"Are you kidding!" she said. "The place will be mobbed. He doesn't even know *my* name."

I relaxed after that and enjoyed most of the service, especially since there wasn't any sermon. The choir sang for forty-five minutes instead.

I got home close to midnight. I was so tired my parents didn't question me. I fell into bed without brushing my teeth.

Are you there God? It's me, Margaret. I just came home from church. I loved the choir—the songs were so beautiful. Still, I didn't really feel you God. I'm more confused than ever. I'm trying hard to understand but I wish you'd help me a little. If only you could give me a hint God. Which religion should I be? Sometimes I wish I'd been born one way or the other.

Grandma came back from her cruise in time to pack up and head for Florida. She said New York had nothing to offer since I was gone. She sent me two postcards a week, called every Friday night and promised to be home before Easter.

Our phone conversations were always the same. I talked first: "Hello, Grandma. . . . Yes, I'm fine. . . . They're fine. . . . School's fine. . . . I miss you too."

Then my father talked: "Hello, Mother. . . . Yes, we're fine. . . . How's the weather down there? . . . Well, it's bound to come out sooner or later. That's why they call it the Sunshine State."

Then my mother talked: "Hello, Sylvia. . . . Yes, Margaret's really fine. . . . Of course I'm sure. . . . Okay—and you take care too."

Then I talked a second time: "Bye, Grandma. See you soon."

During the second week in January Mr. Benedict announced that the sixth-grade girls were going to see a movie on Friday afternoon. The sixth-grade boys were not going to see the movie. At that time they would have a discussion with the boy's gym teacher from the junior high.

Nancy passed me a note. It said, *Here we go—the big deal sex movie.*

When I asked her about it she told me the PTA sponsors it and it's called *What Every Girl Should Know.*

When I went home I told my mother. "We're going to see a movie in school on Friday."

"I know," my mother said. "I got a letter in the mail. It's about menstruation."

"I already *know* all about that."

"I know *you* know," my mother said. "But it's important for *all* the girls to see it in case their mothers haven't told them the facts."

"Oh."

On Friday morning there was a lot of giggling. Finally, at two o'clock, the girls lined up and went to the auditorium. We took up the first three rows of seats. There was a lady on the stage, dressed in a gray suit. She had a big behind. Also, she wore a hat.

"Hello, girls," she said. She clutched a hanky which she waved at us sometimes. "I'm here today to tell you about *What Every Girl Should Know*, brought to you as a courtesy of the Private Lady Company. We'll talk some more after the film." Her voice was smooth, like a radio announcer's.

Then the lights went out and we saw the movie. The narrator of the film pronounced it menstroo-ation. "Remember," the voice said, "it's menstroo-ation." Gretchen, who was next to me, gave me a kick and I kicked Nancy on the other side. We held our hands over our mouths so we wouldn't laugh.

The film told us about the ovaries and explained why girls menstroo-ate. But it didn't tell us how it feels, except to say that it is not painful, which we knew anyway. Also, it didn't really show a girl getting it. It just said how wonderful nature was and how we would soon become women and all that. After the film the lady in the gray suit asked if there were any questions.

Nancy raised her hand and when Gray Suit called on her Nancy said, "How about Tampax?"

Gray Suit coughed into her hanky and said, "We don't advise *internal protection* until you are considerably older."

Then Gray Suit came down from the stage and passed out booklets called *What Every Girl Should Know*. The booklet recommended that we use Private Lady sanitary supplies. It was like one big commercial. I made a mental note never to buy Private Lady things *when* and *if* I ever needed them.

For days after that whenever I looked at Gretchen, Janie or Nancy we'd pretend to be saying menstrooation. We laughed a lot. Mr. Benedict told us we'd have to settle down since we had a lot to learn before we'd be ready for seventh grade.

One week later Gretchen got it. We had a special PTS meeting that afternoon.

"I got it last night. Can you tell?" she asked us.

"Oh, Gretchen! You lucky!" Nancy shrieked. "I was sure I'd be first. I've got more than you!"

"Well, that doesn't mean much," Gretchen said, knowingly.

"How did it happen?" I asked.

"Well, I was sitting there eating my supper when I felt like something was dripping from me."

"Go on—go on," Nancy said.

"Well, I ran to the bathroom, and when I saw what it was I called my mother."

"And?" I asked.

"She yelled that she was eating."

"And?" Janie said.

"Well, I yelled back that it was important."

"So—so—" Nancy prompted.

"So . . . uh . . . she came and I showed her," Gretchen said.

"Then what?" Janie asked.

"Well, she didn't have any stuff in the house. She uses Tampax herself—so she had to call the drugstore and order some pads."

"What'd you do in the meantime?" Janie asked.

"Kept a wash cloth in my pants," Gretchen said.

"Oh—you didn't!" Nancy said, laughing.

"Well, I had to," Gretchen said.

"Okay—so then what?" I asked.

"Well . . . in about an hour the stuff came from the drugstore."

"Then what?" Nancy asked.

"My mother showed me how to attach the pad to the belt. Oh . . . you know . . ."

Nancy was mad. "Look Gretchen, did we or did we

not make a deal to tell each other absolutely everything about getting it?"

"I'm telling you, aren't I?" Gretchen asked.

"Not enough," Nancy said. "What's it *feel* like?"

"Mostly I don't feel anything. Sometimes it feels like it's dripping. It doesn't hurt coming out—but I had some cramps last night."

"Bad ones?" Janie asked.

"Not bad. Just different," Gretchen said. "Lower down, and across my back."

"Does it make you feel older?" I asked.

"Naturally," Gretchen answered. "My mother said now I'll really have to watch what I eat because I've gained too much weight this year. And she said to wash my face well from now on—with soap."

"And that's it?" Nancy said. "The whole story?"

"I'm sorry if I've disappointed you, Nancy. But really, that's all there is to tell. Oh, one thing I forgot. My mother said I may not get it every month yet. Sometimes it takes a while to get regular."

"Are you using that Private Lady stuff?" I asked.

"No, the drugstore sent *Teenage Softies*."

"Well, I guess I'll be next," Nancy said.

Janie and I looked at each other. We guessed so too.

When I went home I told my mother. "Gretchen Potter got her period."

"Did she really?" my mother asked.

"Yes," I said.

"I guess you'll begin soon too."

"How old were you Mom—when you got it?"

"Uh . . . I think I was fourteen."

"*Fourteen!* That's crazy. I'm not waiting until I'm fourteen."

"I'm afraid there's not much you can do about it, Margaret. Some girls menstruate earlier than others. I had a cousin who was sixteen before she started."

"Do you suppose that could happen to me? I'll die if it does!"

"If you don't start by the time you're fourteen I'll take you to the doctor. Now stop worrying!"

"How can I stop worrying when I don't know if I'm going to turn out normal?"

"I promise, you'll turn out normal."

Are you there God? It's me, Margaret. Gretchen, my friend, got her period. I'm so jealous God. I hate myself for being so jealous, but I am. I wish you'd help me just a little. Nancy's sure she's going to get it soon, too. And if I'm last I don't know what I'll do. Oh please God. I just want to be normal.

Nancy and her family went to Washington over Lincoln's birthday weekend. I got a postcard from her before she got back which means she must have mailed it the second she got there. It only had three words on it.

I GOT IT!!!

I ripped the card into tiny shreds and ran to my room. There was something wrong with me. I just knew it. And there wasn't a thing I could do about it. I flopped onto my bed and cried. Next week Nancy would want to tell me all about her period and about how grown up she was. Well, I didn't want to hear her good news!

Are you there God? It's me, Margaret. Life is getting worse every day. I'm going to be the only one who doesn't get it. I know it God. Just like I'm the only one without a religion. Why can't you help me? Haven't I always done what you wanted? Please . . . let me be like everybody else.

My mother took me to Lincoln Center twice. We used Grandma's subscription tickets. It wasn't as much fun as with Grandma, because number one, I didn't get to ride the bus alone, and number two, my mother thought the concert itself was more important than looking at the people. I wrote Grandma a letter.

Dear Grandma,
I miss you. Florida sure sounds like fun.
School is fine. So are Mom and Dad. I am fine
too. I've only had one cold so far and two
viruses. One was the throwing up kind.
I forgot to tell you this over the phone, but when
we went to Lincoln Center there was slush all over
the place so I couldn't sit by the fountain.
I had to wear boots too, and my feet sweated
during the concert. Mom wouldn't let me
take them off, the way you do. It snowed
again yesterday. I'll bet you don't miss that,
do you! But snow is more fun in New Jersey
than in New York. For one thing, it's cleaner.
Love,
Margaret

Grandma wrote back:

Dear Margaret,
I miss you too. Thank you for your nice letter.
I hope when you were sick your mother
took you to a good doctor. If I had been home
I would have asked Dr. Cohen who he
recommends in New Jersey. There must be one
or two good doctors there. You probably
caught cold because you kept your boots on at
Lincoln Center. Your mother should know better!
From now on, take off your boots the way we
always do—no matter what your mother says!
Only don't tell her I said so.
I met a very nice man at my hotel. His name is
Mr. Binamin. He comes from New York too.
We have dinner together and sometimes see
a show. He is a widower with three children
(all married). *They* think he should
get married again. *He* thinks he should get
married again. But I'm not saying anything!
I hope your mother and father will let you
come stay with me during spring vacation.
Would you like that? I'm writing a letter
to ask their permission.
Be careful and dress warmly! Write to me again.
All my love,
Grandma

Dear Grandma,
Mom and Dad say I can probably visit you
during spring vacation, but that it's too
soon to make definite plans. I'm so excited
I could die! I'm counting the days already.
I've never been on a plane, as you know. And
Florida sounds like so much fun! Also, I want
to see what's going on with you and that Mr.
Binamin. You never tell us a thing when you call!
I am fine. The snow melted. Mom is painting
a new picture. This one is of apricots, grapes
and ivy leaves. Did I tell you my friends
Nancy and Gretchen got their periods?
See you soon, I hope.
Love and kisses,
Margaret

17

On the first Sunday in March Nancy invited me to spend the day in New York with her family. Evan brought Moose. It was pretty exciting riding all the way to the city with Moose Freed in the same car, except the Wheelers used their station wagon. The boys sat in the back and Nancy and I were in the middle, so if I wanted to see Moose I had to turn around and if I ride looking backwards like that I get car sick.

We went to Radio City Music Hall. Grandma used to take me there when I was little. My parents always say it's strictly for the tourists. I wanted to sit next to Moose but he and Evan found two seats off by themselves.

After the show the Wheelers took us to the Steak Place for dinner. Nancy and I ordered, then excused ourselves to go to the ladies' room. We were the only two in there, which was lucky for us because there were only two toilets and we both had to go pretty bad. Just as I was finishing up I heard Nancy moan.

"Oh no—oh no—"

"What is it, Nancy?" I asked.

"Oh please—oh no—

"Are you okay?" I banged on the wall separating us.

"Get my mother—quick!" she whispered.

I stood in front of her booth then. "What's wrong?" I tried the door but it was locked. "Let me in."

Nancy started to cry. "Please get my mother."

"Okay. I'm going. I'll be right back."

I raced to our table in the dining room, hoping Nancy wouldn't faint or anything like that before I got back with her mother.

I whispered to Mrs. Wheeler, "Nancy's sick. She's in the bathroom crying and she wants you."

Mrs. Wheeler jumped up and followed me back to the ladies' room. I could hear Nancy sobbing.

"Nancy?" Mrs. Wheeler called, trying the door.

"Oh Mom—I'm so scared! Help me—please."

"The door's locked, Nancy. I can't get in," Mrs. Wheeler said. "You've got to unlock it."

"I can't—I can't—" Nancy cried.

"I could crawl under and open it from the other side," I suggested. "Should I?" I asked Mrs. Wheeler. She nodded.

I gathered my skirt around my legs so it wouldn't drag on the floor and crawled under the door. Nancy's face was buried in her hands. I unlocked the door for Mrs. Wheeler, then waited outside by the sinks. I wondered if Nancy would have to go to the hospital or what. I hoped she didn't have anything catching.

In a few minutes Mrs. Wheeler opened the door a crack and handed me some change. "Margaret," she said, "would you get us a sanitary napkin please?" I must have given her a strange look because she said, "From the dispenser on the wall, dear. Nancy's menstruating."

"Does she always act like that?"

"It's her first time," Mrs. Wheeler explained. "She's frightened." Nancy was still crying and there was a lot of whispering going on.

I couldn't believe it! Nancy, who knew everything! She'd lied to me about her period. She'd never had it before!

I put the change into the machine and pulled the lever. The sanitary napkin popped out in a cardboard box. I handed it to Mrs. Wheeler.

"Nancy, calm down," I heard her mother say. "I can't help you if you don't stop crying."

Suppose I hadn't been along that day? I'd never have found out about Nancy. I almost wished I hadn't.

Finally Nancy and her mother came out of the booth and Mrs. Wheeler suggested that Nancy wash up before coming back to the table. "I'm going to tell the others not to worry," she said. "Don't be too long, girls."

I didn't know what to say. I mean, what can you say when you've just found out your friend's a liar!

Nancy washed her hands and face. I handed her two paper towels to dry herself. "Are you okay?" I asked. I felt kind of sorry for Nancy then. I want my period too, but not enough to lie about it.

Nancy faced me. "Margaret, please don't tell."

"Oh Nancy . . . "

"I mean it. I'd die if the others knew. Promise you won't tell about me," she begged.

"I won't."

"I thought I had it that time. You know . . . I didn't just make it all up. It was a mistake."

"Okay," I said.

"You won't tell?"

"I said I wouldn't."

We walked back to the table and joined the others for dinner. Our steaks were just being served. I sat next to Moose. He smelled very nice. I wondered if he shaved because the nice smell reminded me of my father's after-shave lotion. I got to touch his hand a couple of times because he was a lefty and I'm a righty so now and then we'd bump. He said he always has that trouble at round tables. He was definitely number one in my Boy Book, even if nobody knew it but me.

I could only finish half of my steak. The Wheelers took the other half home in a doggie bag. I knew they didn't have a dog but naturally I didn't tell the waitress.

Are you there God? It's me, Margaret. Nancy Wheeler is a big fake. She makes up stories! I'll never be able to trust her again. I will wait to find out from you if I am normal or not. If you would like to give me a sign, fine. If not, I'll try to be patient. All I ask is that I don't get it in school because if I had to tell Mr. Benedict I know I would die. Thank you God.

18

On March eighth I was twelve years old. The first thing I did was sniff under my arms, the way my mother does. Nothing! I didn't smell a thing. Still, now that I was twelve, I decided I'd better use deodorant, just in case. I went into my parents' bathroom and reached for my mother's roll-on. When I got dressed I went down to the kitchen for breakfast.

"Happy Birthday, Margaret!" my mother sang, bending over to kiss me while I was drinking my orange juice.

"Thank you, Mom," I said. "I used your deodorant."

My mother laughed. "You don't have to use mine. I'll get you your own."

"You will?" I asked.

"Sure, if you want to use it regularly."

"Well, I think I'd better. I'm twelve now, you know."

"I know—I know." My mother smiled at me while she cut some banana onto my cereal.

Grandma sent me a hundred-dollar savings bond as she does every year—plus three new sweaters with MADE EXPRESSLY FOR YOU . . . BY GRANDMA labels in them, a new bathing suit and an airline ticket to Florida! Round trip, leaving from Newark Airport at noon on April fourth. Was I excited!

In school Mr. Benedict shook my hand and wished me a lot of good luck in the coming year. He led the class in singing "Happy Birthday" to me. Nancy, Janie and Gretchen chipped in and bought me the new Mice Men record album. They gave it to me at lunch. Nancy mailed me a separate birthday card signed, *A million thanks to the best friend a girl could ever have.* I guess she was still scared I'd give away her secret.

That afternoon Mr. Benedict announced that for the next three weeks a part of each school day would be devoted to committee work. We were going to do projects on different countries. Janie, Nancy, Gretchen and I gave each other looks saying we'd work together, of course.

But that sneaky Miles J. Benedict! He said that since he wanted us to work with people we hadn't worked with before he had made up the committees already. Well, that's a first-year teacher for you! Didn't he know that was a bad idea? Didn't he know he was supposed to let us form our own committees? Teachers never come right out and say they've picked who you should work with. It's bad enough that they fool you a lot by pretending to let you choose a subject when they know all along what you're going to do. But this was ridiculous!

I guess Mr. Benedict didn't think it was ridiculous because he was already reading out names of committees. Each group had four kids in it. Two boys and two girls, with one group left over that had three girls. I really couldn't believe it when he read my group. Norman Fishbein, Philip Leroy, Laura Danker and me! I glanced sideways at Janie. She rolled her eyes at me. I raised my eyebrow back at her.

Mr. Benedict asked us to rearrange our desks into our groups. I was going to have to talk to Laura Danker! There would be no way of getting out of it. I was also going to be spending a lot of time with Philip Leroy, which was pretty exciting to think about.

The first thing Philip did after we moved our desks together was to sing to me.

"Happy Birthday to you,
You live in a zoo,
You look like a monkey,
And you smell like one too!"

Then he pinched me on the arm—really hard! Enough to make tears come to my eyes. He said, "That's pinch to grow an inch. And you know where you need that inch!"

I knew it was just a joke. I knew I shouldn't take it seriously. For one thing, I did not smell like a monkey. I was wearing deodorant! And for another thing, it was none of Philip Leroy's business whether or not I needed to grow an inch *anywhere!* As far as I was concerned, Nancy could have him. They deserved each other.

To make matters worse I had to sit facing Laura Danker. I hated her. I hated her for being so big and beautiful and having all the boys stare at her, including Mr. Benedict. Also, I hated her because she knew she was normal and I didn't know a thing about me! I hated Mr. Benedict too—for sticking me with Norman Fishbein. Norman was such a drip!

So all in all my birthday, which started out to be the most perfect day of my life, ended up being pretty rotten. I couldn't wait for spring vacation to come. The only good thing I had to look forward to was my trip to Florida. I was sick of school.

At home my mother said she'd never seen me in such a bad mood. The mood lasted the whole three weeks of that dumb committee project. To top off everything else our group voted three to one to report on Belgium. I wanted a more exciting country, like France or Spain. But I lost.

So I ate, breathed and slept Belgium for three weeks. Philip Leroy was a lousy worker. I found that out right away. All he did was fool around. During project time, while Laura, Norman and I were busy looking things up in reference books, Philip was busy drawing funny faces in his notebook. On two days he snuck comic books inside his notebook and read them instead. Norman Fishbein tried hard but he was so slow! And I couldn't stand the way he read with his lips moving. Laura was a good worker. But of course, I never told her that *I* thought so.

During the third week of Project Belgium Laura and I got permission to stay after school and work in the library. We needed more time with the encyclopedias. My mother was going to pick me up in front of school at four-thirty. Laura was going to walk from school to church because she had to go to Confession.

Now that really started me thinking. For one thing, I never knew she was Catholic. For another, I wondered what she said in Confession. I mean, did she talk about what she did with boys? And if she did, what did the priest say to her? Did she go to Confession every time she did something bad? Or did she save it all up and go once a month?

I was so busy thinking about Laura and the Confessional that I nearly forgot about Belgium. And probably I never would have said anything at all if it hadn't been for Laura. She picked on me first. So she was really to blame for the whole thing.

"You're copying that straight out of the *World Book* word for word," she whispered to me.

"So?"

"Well, you can't do that," she explained. "You're supposed to read it and then write about it in your own words. Mr. Benedict will *know* if you've copied."

Normally I don't copy word for word. I know the rules as well as Laura. But I was busy thinking about other things and anyway, who did Laura think she was giving orders like that? Big shot!

So I said: "Oh, you think you're so great, don't you!"

And she said: "This has nothing to do with being great."

And I said: "I know all about you anyway!"

And she said: "What's *that* supposed to mean?"

And the librarian said: "Girls—let's be more quiet."

And then Laura went back to work. But I didn't.

"I heard all about you and Moose Freed," I whispered.

Laura put down her pencil and looked at me. "You heard *what* about me and Moose Freed?"

"Oh—about how you and Evan and Moose go behind the A&P," I said.

"What would I do *that* for?" Laura asked.

She was really thick! "I don't know what *you* do it for. But I know why *they* do it . . . they do it so they can *feel* you or something and *you* let them!"

She shut the encyclopedia hard and stood up. Her face was burning red and I saw a blue vein stick out in her neck. "You filthy liar! *You little pig!*" Nobody ever called me such names in my whole life.

Laura scooped up her books and her coat and ran out of the library. I grabbed my things and followed her.

I was really being awful. And I hadn't even planned it. I sounded like Nancy. That's when it hit me that for all I knew Nancy made up that story about Laura. Or maybe Moose and Evan made it up just to brag. Yes, I bet they did! Moose was a big liar too!

"Hey Laura! Wait up," I called.

She walked fast—probably because her legs were so long. I chased her. When I finally caught up to her I could hardly breathe. Laura kept walking and wouldn't look at me. I didn't blame her. I walked alongside her. I took four steps to every two of hers.

"Look," I told her. "I'm not saying it's wrong to do those things."

"I think it's disgusting that you all pick on me because I'm big!" Laura said, sniffling.

I wanted to tell her to blow her nose. "I didn't mean to insult you," I said. "You're the one who started it."

"Me? That's a good one! You think it's such a great game to make fun of me, don't you?"

"No," I said.

"Don't you think I know all about *you* and your friends? Do you think it's any fun to be the biggest kid in the class?"

"I don't know," I said. "I never thought about it."

"Well, try thinking about it. Think about how you'd feel if you had to wear a bra in fourth grade and how everybody laughed and how you always had to cross your arms in front of you. And about how the boys called you dirty names just because of how you looked."

I thought about it. "I'm sorry, Laura," I said.

"I'll bet!"

"I really am. If you want to know the truth . . . well, I wish I looked more like you than like me."

"I'd gladly trade places with you. Now, I'm going to Confession." She walked on mumbling something about how the wrong ones always confessed.

And I thought, maybe she's right. Maybe I was the one who should confess. I followed Laura to her church. It was only two blocks from school. I still had half an hour before my mother was due. I crossed the street and hid behind a bush watching Laura climb the steps and disappear into the church.

Then I crossed back to the other side of the street and ran up the brick steps. I held open the front door and looked inside. I didn't see Laura. I stepped into the church and tiptoed up the aisle.

It was so quiet. I wondered what would happen if I decided to scream; of course I knew I wouldn't, but I couldn't help wondering about how a scream would sound in there.

I was really hot in my heavy coat, but I didn't take it off. After a while I saw Laura come out of a door and I crouched down behind a row of seats so she wouldn't see me. She never even glanced my way. I thought it didn't take her very long to confess.

I felt weird. My legs were getting weak. As soon as Laura left the church I stood up. I meant to leave too. I had to meet my mother back at school. But instead of walking to the front of the church and outside, I headed the other way.

I stood in front of the door that Laura came from. What was inside? I opened it a little. There was nobody there. It looked like a wooden phone booth. I stepped in and closed the door behind me. I waited for something to happen. I didn't know what I was supposed to do, so I just sat there.

Finally I heard a voice. "Yes, my child."

At first I thought it was God. I really and truly

thought it was, and my heart started to pound like crazy and I was all sweaty inside my coat and sort of dizzy too. But then I realized it was only the priest in the booth next to mine. He couldn't see me and I couldn't see him but we could hear each other. Still, I didn't say anything.

"Yes, my child," he said again.

"I . . . I . . . uh . . . uh . . . " I began.

"Yes?" the priest asked me.

"I'm sorry," I whispered.

I flung open the door and ran down the aisle and out of the church. I made my way back to school, crying, feeling horribly sick and scared stiff I would throw up. Then I saw my mother waiting in the car and I got in the back and explained I was feeling terrible. I stretched out on the seat. My mother drove home and I didn't have to tell her any of the awful things I'd done because she thought I was sick for real.

Later that night she brought a bowl of soup to my room and she sat on the edge of my bed while I ate it. She said I must have had a virus or something and she was glad I was feeling better but I didn't have to go to school tomorrow if I didn't feel like it. Then she turned out the light and kissed me goodnight.

Are you there God? It's me, Margaret. I did an awful thing today. Just awful! I'm definitely the most horrible person who ever lived and I really don't deserve anything good to happen to me. I picked on Laura Danker. Just because I felt mean I took it all out on her. I really hurt Laura's feelings. Why did you let me do that? I've been looking for you God. I looked in temple. I looked in church. And today, I looked for you when I wanted to confess. But you weren't there. I didn't feel you at all. Not the way I do when I talk to you at night .Why God? Why do I only feel you when I'm alone?

20

A week before spring vacation the letter came. Only it wasn't from Grandma and it wasn't about my trip to Florida. It was from Mary and Paul Hutchins, my other grandparents. Now that was really strange because since they disowned my mother when she got married naturally they never wrote to her. My father, having no kind thoughts about them, really hit the roof.

"How did they get our address? Answer that one simple question please! Just how did they get our address?"

My mother practically whispered her answer. "I sent them a Christmas card. That's how."

My father hollered. "I can't believe you, Barbara! After fourteen years you sent *them* a Christmas card?"

"I was feeling sentimental. So I sent a card. I didn't write anything on it. Just our names."

My father shook the letter at my mother. "So now, after fourteen years—*fourteen years*, Barbara! Now they change their minds?"

"They want to see us. That's all."

"They want to see *you*, not me! They want to see Margaret! To make sure she doesn't have horns!"

"Herb! Stop it! You're being ridiculous——"

"*I'm being ridiculous!* That's funny, Barbara. That's very funny."

"You know what I think?" I asked them. "I think you're both being ridiculous!" I ran out of the kitchen and stormed up the stairs to my room. I slammed the door. I hated it when they had a fight in front of me. Why didn't they know how much I hated it! Didn't they know how awful they sounded? I could still hear them, shouting and carrying on. I put my hands over my ears while I crossed the room to my record player. Then I took one hand off one ear and turned on my Mice Men record as loud as it would go. There—that was much better.

A few minutes later my bedroom door opened. My father walked straight to my record player and snapped it off. My mother held the letter in her hand. Her eyes were red. I didn't say anything.

My father paced up and down. "Margaret," he finally said. "This concerns you. I think before we do or say anything else you ought to read the letter from your grandparents. Barbara . . . " He held out his hand.

My mother handed the letter to my father and he handed it to me. The handwriting was slanty and perfect, the way it is in third grade when you're learning script. I sat down on my bed.

Dear Barbara,
Your father and I have been thinking about

122

you a lot. We are growing old. I guess you find
that hard to believe, but we are. Suddenly, more
than anything else we want to see our only
daughter. We wonder if it is possible that we
made a mistake fourteen years ago. We have
discussed this situation with our minister and
dear friend, Reverend Baylor. You remember
him dear, don't you. My goodness, he christened
you when you were a tiny baby. He says it's
never too late to try again. So your father and I
are flying East for a week and hope that you will
let us visit you and get to know our granddaughter, Margaret Ann. Flight details are
enclosed.
Your mother,
Mary Hutchins

What a sickening letter! No wonder my father was
mad. It didn't even mention him.

I handed the letter back to my father, but I didn't
say anything because I didn't know what I was supposed to say.

"They're coming on April fifth," my father said.

"Oh, then I won't see them after all," I said,
brightening. "I leave for Florida on the fourth."

My mother looked at my father.

"Well," I said. "Isn't that right? I leave for Florida
on the fourth!"

They still didn't say anything and after a minute I

knew—I *knew* I wasn't going to Florida! And then I had plenty to say. Plenty!

"I don't want to see them," I shouted. "It isn't fair! I want to go to Florida and stay with Grandma. Daddy—*please!*"

"Don't look at me," my father said quietly. "It's not my fault. I didn't send them a Christmas card."

"Mom!" I cried. "You can't do this to me. You can't! It's not fair—it's not!" I hated my mother. I really did. She was so stupid. What did she have to go and send them a dumb old card for!

"Come on, Margaret. It's not the end of the world," my mother said, putting her arm around me. "You'll go to Florida another time."

I wriggled away from her as my father said, "Somebody better call Sylvia and tell her the change in plans."

"I'll put the call through and Margaret can tell her now," my mother said.

"Oh no!" I shouted. "*You* tell her. It's not my idea!"

"All right," my mother said quietly. "All right, I will."

I followed my parents into their bedroom. My mother picked up the phone and placed a person-to-person call to Grandma at her hotel. After a few minutes she said, "Hello, Sylvia . . . It's Barbara. . . . Nothing's wrong. . . . Everything's fine. . . . Yes, really. . . . Of course I'm sure. . . . It's just that Margaret won't be able to visit you after all. . . . Of course she's here . . . she's standing right next to me. . . . Yes, you can talk to her. . . ."

My mother held the phone out toward me. But I shook my head and refused to take it. So she covered the mouthpiece and whispered, "Grandma thinks you're sick. You've got to tell her you're all right."

I took the phone. "Grandma," I said, "it's Margaret."

I heard Grandma catch her breath.

"Nothing's wrong, Grandma. . . . No, I'm not sick. . . . Nobody's sick. . . . Of course I'm sure. . . . But I do want to come, Grandma. I just can't." I felt the tears in my eyes. My throat hurt when I swallowed. My mother motioned for me to tell Grandma the rest of the story. "I can't come to Florida because we're having company that week." Now my voice sounded very high and squeaky.

Grandma asked me, what company?

"My other grandparents," I said. "You know, Mom's mother and father. . . . Nobody invited them exactly . . . but Mom sent them a Christmas card with our new address and now we got a letter saying they're coming and they want to see me. . . . Well, I know you want to see me too. And I want to see you but Mom won't let me. . . ."

Then I started to cry for real and my mother took the phone.

"We're all sorry, Sylvia. It's just one of those things. Margaret understands. I hope you do too. Thank

125

you, Sylvia. I knew you would. . . . Yes, Herb's fine. I'll put him on. Just a minute." I ran upstairs while my father said, "Hello, mother."

Are you there God? It's me, Margaret. I'm so miserable! Everything is wrong. Absolutely everything! I guess this is my punishment for being a horrible person. I guess you think it's only fair for me to suffer after what I did to Laura. Isn't that right God? But I've always tried to do what you wanted. Really, I have. Please don't let them come God. Make something happen so I can go to Florida anyway. Please . . .

21

That week my mother went crazy cleaning the house, while I waited for something to happen. I thought it would be a telegram saying they weren't able to come after all. I was sure God only wanted to punish me for a little while. Not for the whole spring vacation.

"Cheer up, Margaret," my mother said over dinner. "Things are never as bad as they seem."

"How can you be glad they're coming?" I asked. "After all those stories you've told me about them—how?"

"I want to show them how well I've managed for fourteen years without their help. And I want them to see my wonderful family."

My father said, "You can't expect Margaret to be overjoyed when her plans have been changed at the last minute."

"Look, Herb," my mother said. "I haven't forgiven my parents. You know that. I never will. But they're coming. I can't say no. Try to understand . . . both of you . . . please."

My mother hadn't ever asked me to do that before. Usually it was me asking her to try to understand.

My father kissed her on the cheek as she cleared away the dishes. He promised to make the best of it. I promised too. My mother kissed us both and said she had the best family in the world.

On April fifth my mother and I drove to Newark Airport to meet them. My father didn't come. He thought it would be better if he stayed at home and greeted them there.

All the way to the airport my mother briefed me. "Margaret, I'm not trying to make excuses for my mother and father. But I want you to know that your grandparents have their beliefs too. And fourteen years ago . . . well . . . they did what they thought was right. Even though we know it was cruel. Their beliefs were that important to them. Am I making any sense to you?"

"Some," I said.

When they announced the arrival of flight #894 from Toledo I followed my mother to the gate. I knew it was them right away. I knew it by the way they walked down the airplane stairs, clutching each other. And when they got closer I knew it by my grandmother's shoes—black with laces and fat heels—old lady shoes. My grandfather had white hair around the edges and none on top. He was shorter and fatter than my grandmother.

They looked around a bit before my mother called out, "Here we are—over here."

They walked toward us, growing more excited as they recognized my mother. She gave each of them a short hug. I just stood there feeling dumb until my grandmother said, "And this must be Margaret Ann." When she said it I noticed the cross around her neck. It was the biggest one I ever saw. And it sparkled!

I didn't want them to touch me. And maybe they could tell, because when my grandmother bent over, as if to kiss me, I stiffened. I didn't mean to. It just happened.

I think my mother knew how I felt because she told them we'd better see about the luggage.

When we got home my father met us at our front door and carried in their suitcases. They had two of them. Both brown and both new.

"Hello, Herb," my grandmother said.

"Hello, Mrs. Hutchins," my father answered.

I thought how funny it was for my father to call her "Mrs."

My grandfather shook hands with my father. "You're looking well, Herb," he said.

My father pressed his lips together but finally managed to say, "Thank you."

I thought, this is harder on my father than it is on me!

My mother and I showed my grandparents to their

room. Then my mother went down to see about dinner. I said, "If there's anything you need, just ask me."

"Thank you, Margaret Ann," my grandmother said. She had a funny way of scrunching up her mouth.

"You don't have to call me Margaret Ann," I said. "Nobody does. Just Margaret is fine."

My mother really made a fancy dinner. The kind she has when she's entertaining friends and I'm sent to bed early. We had flowers on the table and a hired lady to wash the dishes.

My mother changed into a new dress and her hair looked nice too. She didn't look like her parents at all. My grandmother changed her dress too, but she still had the cross around her neck.

At dinner we all tried hard to have a conversation. My mother and my grandmother talked about old friends from Ohio and who was doing what these days. My grandfather said mostly, "Please pass the butter . . . please pass the salt."

Naturally I used my best possible manners. In the middle of the roast beef course my grandfather knocked over his water glass and my grandmother gave him a sharp look, but my mother said water couldn't possible hurt anything. The lady from the kitchen wiped it up.

During dessert my mother explained to my grandparents that she had just ordered all new living room furniture and she was sorry they wouldn't be able to see it. I knew she hadn't ordered anything yet, but I didn't tell.

After dinner we sat around in the den and my grandfather asked my father such questions as:

GRANDFATHER: "Are you still in the insurance business?"

FATHER: "Yes."

GRANDFATHER: "Do you invest in the stock market?"

FATHER: "Occasionally."

GRANDFATHER: "This is a pretty nice house."

FATHER: "Thank you. We think so too."

While my grandmother talked to my mother about:

GRANDMOTHER: "We were in California over Thanksgiving."

MOTHER: "Oh?"

GRANDMOTHER: "Yes, your brother has a wonderful wife."

MOTHER: "I'm glad."

GRANDMOTHER: "If only they were blessed with a child. You know, they're thinking of adopting."

MOTHER: "I hope they do. Everyone should have a child to love."

GRANDMOTHER: "Yes, I know. . . . I've always wanted dozens of grandchildren, but Margaret's all I've got."

Then my mother excused herself to pay the lady in the kitchen, who signaled that her taxi was waiting out front. So my grandmother turned to me.

"Do you like school?" she asked.

"Most of the time," I said.

"Do you get good marks?"

"Pretty good," I said.

"How do you do in Sunday school?"

My mother came back into the den then and sat down next to me.

"I don't go to Sunday school," I said.

"You don't?"

"No."

"Father . . . (That's what Grandmother called Grandfather. He called her "Mother.")

"What is it, Mother?" Grandfather said.

"Margaret doesn't go to Sunday school." Grandmother shook her head and played with her cross.

"Look," my mother said, trying a smile. "You know we don't practice any religion."

Here it comes, I thought. I wanted to leave the room then but I felt like I was glued to my seat.

"We hoped by now you'd changed your minds about religion," Grandfather said.

"Especially for Margaret's sake," Grandmother added. "A person's got to have religion."

"Let's not get into a philosophical discussion," my father said, annoyed. He sent my mother a warning look across the room.

Grandfather laughed. "I'm not being a philosopher, Herb."

"Look," my mother explained, "we're letting Margaret choose her own religion when she's grown."

"If she wants to!" my father said, defiantly.

"Nonsense!" Grandmother said. "A person doesn't choose religion."

"A person's born to it!" Grandfather boomed.

Grandmother smiled at last and gave a small laugh. "So Margaret is Christian!" she announced, like we all should have known.

"Please . . ." my mother said. "Margaret could just as easily be Jewish. Don't you see—if you keep this up you're going to spoil everything."

"I don't mean to upset you, dear," Grandmother told my mother. "But a child is always the religion of the mother. And you, Barbara, were born Christian. You were baptized. It's that simple."

"Margaret is nothing!" my father stormed. "And I'll thank you for ending this discussion right now."

I didn't want to listen anymore. How could they talk that way in front of me! Didn't they know I was a real person—with feelings of my own!

"Margaret," Grandmother said, touching my sleeve. "It's not too late for you, dear. You're still God's child. Maybe while I'm visiting I could take you to church and talk to the minister. He might be able to straighten things out."

"Stop it!" I hollered, jumping up. "All of you! Just stop it! I can't stand another minute of listening to you. Who needs religion? Who! Not me . . . I don't need it. I don't even need God!" I ran out of the den and up to my room.

I heard my mother say, "Why did you have to start? Now you've ruined everything!"

I was never going to talk to God again. What did he want from me anyway? I was through with him and his religions! And I was never going to set foot in the Y or the Jewish Community Center—*never*.

22

The next morning I stayed in my room. I wouldn't even go down for breakfast. I caught myself starting to say, *Are you there God*, but then I remembered that I wasn't talking to him anymore. I wondered if he would strike me down. Well, if he wanted to, that was his business!

By afternoon I couldn't stand being in the house, so I asked my mother to drive me downtown to meet Janie for a movie. My mother agreed that I needed to get away for a few hours. Janie and I met at the drugstore on the corner, across the street from the movie theater. We were twenty minutes early so we went into the drugstore to look around. Mostly we liked to inspect the sanitary napkin display.

After a few minutes of looking, I whispered to Janie, "Let's buy a box." It was something I'd thought about for a while, but wasn't ever brave enough to do. Today I was feeling brave. I thought, so what if God's mad at me. Who cares? I even tested him by crossing the street in the middle *and* against the light. Nothing happened.

"Buy it for what?" Janie asked.

"Just in case," I told her.

"You mean to keep at home?"

"Sure. Why not?"

"I don't know. My mother might not like it," Janie said.

"So don't tell her."

"But what if she sees it?"

"It'll be in a bag. You can say it's school supplies," I said. "Do you have enough money?"

"Yes."

"Okay. Now, what kind should we buy?" I asked.

"How about *Teenage Softies*?" Janie said. "That's the kind Gretchen uses."

"Okay." I took a box of *Teenage Softies* off the shelf. "Well, go ahead," I said to Janie. "Take yours."

"Okay, okay." Janie took a box too.

"We need a belt to go with it," I said, getting braver by the minute.

"You're right. Which kind?" Janie asked.

"I like that one. It's pink," I told her, pointing to a small box with a pretty girl's picture on it.

"Okay, I'll take that one too," Janie said, reaching.

We walked to the check-out counter with our stuff and walked away just as fast when we saw that there was a boy behind the cash register.

"I can't go through with it," Janie whispered. She put her boxes back on the shelf. "I'm scared."

"Don't be a dope. What's to be . . ." I was interrupted by a saleslady in a blue doctor's coat.

"Can I help you, girls?" she asked.

Janie shook her head but I said, "We'd like these please." I took Janie's boxes back off the shelf and showed the saleslady what we'd selected.

"Fine, girls. Take them up to the cash register and Max will wrap them for you."

Janie didn't move. She looked like she was cemented to the floor. She had this dumb expression on her face —between crying and smiling. So I grabbed her boxes and headed for Max and the cash register. I plopped everything down in front of him and just stood there not looking at his face and not saying anything either. He added it all up and I motioned to Janie to give me her money. Then I said, "Two bags, please." Max took my money, gave me some change, which I didn't bother to count, and presented me with two brown bags. That was all there was to it! You'd think he sold that kind of stuff every day of the week.

When I got home from the movies my mother asked, "What's that package?"

I said, "School supplies."

I went to my room with my purchases. I sat down on my bed staring at the box of *Teenage Softies*. I hoped God was watching. Let him see I could get along fine without him! I opened the box and took out one pad. I held it for a long time.

Then I took the pink belt out of its box and held that too. Finally I got up and went to my closet. It was dark in there. Especially with the door closed. I wished I had a huge walk-in closet with a light and a lock. But I managed anyway. I got the pink belt around me and attached the pad to it. I wanted to find out how it would feel. Now I knew. I liked it. I thought about sleeping in my belt and pad that night, but decided against it. If there was a fire my secret might be discovered. So I took off the belt and pad, put them back in their boxes and hid them in my bottom desk drawer. My mother never checks there because the mess makes her positively sick!

The next morning my grandparents announced they were moving on to New York.

"You told me a week!" my mother said. "You said you were coming for a week!"

"We did say that," my grandfather told her. "But we've decided to spend the rest of the week in New York, at a hotel."

"I see," my mother said.

My father hid behind his newspaper but I saw the big smile. All I could think of was that they ruined my trip to Florida and now they weren't even staying. It wasn't fair! It was really a cheat!

When my mother got back from driving them to the bus my father said, "How much do you want to bet it was a trip to New York all the time. They just stopped in to see you because it was convenient."

"I don't believe that!" my mother said.

"Well, I believe it," my father said.

"They ruined my vacation," I said.

Nobody answered me.

That night the doorbell rang at eight. We were in the den. I said I'd see who was there. I opened the front door.

"Grandma!" I screamed. I threw my arms around her. "What are you doing home?"

"If Mohammed doesn't come to the mountain—the mountain comes to Mohammed."

I laughed, knowing that I was Mohammed and that Grandma was the mountain. There was a man standing next to Grandma. Grandma turned to him. "Morris," she said. "This is my Margaret."

Then Grandma closed the front door and told me, "Margaret darling, this is Mr. Morris Binamin."

"Rhymes with cinnamon," he said to me.

I smiled.

Grandma looked marvelous—very tan and pale blonde. Mr. Binamin had a lot of silver hair, a moustache to match, and black-rimmed eyeglasses. He was tan too. He held Grandma's arm.

"Where are they?" Grandma asked.

"Mom and Dad are in the den," I said.

"With your other grandparents?"

"No . . . they're gone."

"Gone!" Grandma cried. "But I thought they were staying all week."

"We thought so too," I said.

"But Morris and I came especially to see them."

"You did!" I said. "How come?"

Grandma and Mr. Binamin gave each other a secret look. "Well . . . we thought you might need our support."

"Oh Grandma! I can manage just fine by myself."

"I know you can. You're my Margaret, aren't you? Tell me—did they try anything?"

"Like what?" I asked.

"You know," Grandma said. "Church business."

"Well . . . kind of," I admitted.

"I knew it!" Grandma cried. "Didn't I tell you?" she asked Mr. Binamin.

Mr. Binamin shook his head. "You had them pegged right all the time, Sylvia," he said.

"Just remember, Margaret . . . no matter what they said . . . you're a Jewish girl."

"No I'm not!" I argued. "I'm nothing, and you know it! I don't even believe in God!"

"Margaret!" Grandma said, "Don't ever talk like that about God."

"Why not?" I asked. "It's true!" I wanted to ask God did he hear that! But I wasn't speaking to him and I guess he knew it!

By that time my mother and father were in the living room and Grandma was making the introductions.

My parents gave Mr. Binamin the once-over and he was pretty busy sizing them up too.

Then my mother made coffee and served warm Danish. She offered me some milk and ginger snaps but I wasn't hungry. I wanted to get out of there so I yawned very loud without covering my mouth.

"Margaret dear, if you're so tired, why don't you go up to bed," Grandma said.

"I think I will. Goodnight, everybody."

Sometimes Grandma is almost as bad as everybody else. As long as she loves me and I love her, what difference does religion make?

Mr. Benedict announced that our individual reports on our year-long project would be due next Friday. They wouldn't be graded so we were to be completely honest and not worry about pleasing him. He hoped we had each learned something of value. On Thursday night I wrote a letter.

May 25

Dear Mr. Benedict,
I have conducted a year-long experiment in
religion. I have not come to any conclusions
about what religion I want to be when
I grow up—if I want to be any special
religion at all.
I have read three books on this subject.
They are: *Modern Judaism*, *A History of
Christianity*, and *Catholicism—Past and Present*.
I went to church services at the First
Presbyterian Church of Farbrook. I went to
the United Methodist Church of Farbrook on
Christmas Eve. I attended Temple Israel of
New York City on Rosh Hashanah, which is a
Jewish holiday. I went to Confession at

Saint Bartholomew Church, but I had to leave
the Confessional because I didn't know what
to say. I have not tried being a Buddhist or
a Moslem because I don't know any people of
these religions.
I have not really enjoyed my religious experiments
very much and I don't think I'll make up my mind
one way or the other for a long time. I don't
think a person can decide to be a certain religion
just like that. It's like having to choose your
own name. You think about it a long time and
then you keep changing your mind.
If I should ever have children I will tell
them what religion they are so they can start
learning about it at an early age. Twelve is very
late to learn.
Sincerely,
Margaret Ann Simon

On Friday everybody handed in a thick booklet with
a decorated cover. All I had was the letter. I couldn't
put that in with the pile of booklets. I was too embar-
rassed. It looked like I hadn't done any work at all.

When the bell rang I sat at my desk while everyone
else filed out of the room.

When Mr. Benedict looked up he said, "Yes, Margaret?"

I walked to his desk with my letter.

"I didn't hand in a booklet," I said.

"Oh?"

"I, uh . . . I wrote you a letter instead." I handed it to him, then stood there while he read it.

"I really tried, Mr. Benedict. I'm—I'm sorry. I wanted to do better." I knew I was going to cry. I couldn't say anything else. So I ran out of the classroom.

I got to the Girls' Room before the tears came. I could still hear Mr. Benedict calling, "Margaret— Margaret—" I didn't pay any attention. I splashed cold water on my face. Then I walked home slowly by myself.

What was wrong with me anyway? When I was eleven I hardly ever cried. Now anything and everything could start me bawling. I wanted to talk it over with God. But I wasn't about to let him know that, even though I missed him.

On June seventeenth the PTA gave us a farewell party in the gym and none of the sixth-grade girls wore socks. I wore my first pair of sheer stockings and got my first run in them one hour later. All I could think of was I'd be in seventh grade in September and I was growing up. My mind knew it—even if my body didn't.

The party in the gym was a lot like the Thanksgiving square dance. Mrs. Wheeler and Mrs. Fishbein were chaperones but this time they were dressed in regular clothes.

Our class presented Mr. Benedict with a pair of silver cufflinks that Gretchen's mother had gotten wholesale. He seemed very pleased, because he cleared his throat a lot and sounded like he didn't know what to say except thank you—and that although we hadn't started out to be the greatest sixth grade in the world, we'd come a long way. And thanks to us, next year, he'd be an experienced teacher—*very experienced!* Then we all laughed and some of the girls cried but I didn't.

Nancy, Gretchen, Janie and I had lunch downtown by ourselves and talked about how it would feel to go to Junior High. Janie was afraid she wouldn't be able to find her way around and she'd get lost. Gretchen said probably the teachers would all be mean and Nancy said suppose we weren't in any classes together and then we all went home and cried.

Later that day my mother started packing my camp trunk. I watched her put the stacks of shorts and polos into it. Then I heard the lawn mower. Moose was back. First I got excited about seeing him and then I got mad, thinking about Laura and those stories he helped spread around.

I ran downstairs and outside and yelled, "Hey Moose!" He didn't hear me because the mower made too much noise. So I ran over to where he was cutting and I stood right in his way so he'd have to notice me and I shouted again. "Hey Moose!"

He shut off the mower. "You're in my way," he said.

"I want to tell you something," I said.

"Go ahead."

I put my hands on my hips. "You know what Moose! You're a liar! I don't believe you ever took Laura Danker behind the A&P."

"Who said I did?"

"What do you mean who said it!"

"Well, who?"

"Nancy told me that Evan told her that you and Evan——" I stopped. I sounded like an idiot.

Moose shook his head at me. "You always believe everything you hear about other people?" he asked.

I didn't know what to say.

Moose kept talking. "Well, next time, don't believe it unless you see it! Now if you'll move out of my way, I've got things to do!"

I didn't move. "You know what Moose?" I asked. "What now?"

"I'm sorry I thought you were a liar."

"You know what Margaret?" Moose asked me.

"No, what?"

"You're still in my way!"

I jumped away and Moose turned the mower on again. I heard him singing his favorite song—about the Erie Canal.

I went back into the house. I had to go to the bathroom. I was thinking about Moose and about how I liked to stand close to him. I was thinking that I was glad he wasn't a liar and I was happy that he cut our grass. Then I looked down at my underpants and I couldn't believe it. There was blood on them. Not a lot—but enough. I really hollered, "*Mom—hey Mom —come quick!*"

When my mother got to the bathroom she said, "What is it? What's the matter?"

"I got it," I told her.

"Got what?"

I started to laugh and cry at the same time. "My period. I've got my period!" My nose started running and I reached for a tissue.

"Are you sure, Margaret?" my mother asked.

"Look—look at this," I said, showing her my underpants.

"My God! You've really got it. My little girl!" Then her eyes filled up and she started sniffling too. "Wait a minute—I've got the equipment in the other room. I was going to put it in your camp trunk, just in case."

"You were?"

"Yes. Just in case." She left the bathroom.

When she came back I asked her, "Is it that Private Lady stuff?"

"No, I got you *Teenage Softies.*"

"Good," I said.

"Now look, Margaret—here's how you do it. The belt goes around your waist and the pad——"

"Mom," I said. "I've been practicing in my room for two months!"

Then my mother and I laughed together and she said, "In that case, I guess I'll wait in the other room."

I locked the bathroom door and attached a *Teenage Softie* to the little hooks on my pink belt. Then I got dressed and looked at myself in the mirror. Would anyone know my secret? Would it show? Would Moose, for instance, know if I went back outside to talk to him? Would my father know it right away when he came home for dinner? I had to call Nancy and Gretchen and Janie right away. Poor Janie! She'd be the last of the PTS's to get it. And I'd been so sure it would be me! How about that! Now I am growing for sure. Now I am almost a woman!

Are you still there God? It's me, Margaret. I know you're there God. I know you wouldn't have missed this for anything! Thank you God. Thanks an awful lot. . . .

Also by JUDY BLUME

IGGIE'S HOUSE

THEN AGAIN, MAYBE I WON'T

IT'S NOT THE END OF THE WORLD

DEENIE